"Give Lily to Storm!"

Tristan ran hard, keeping pace as Avery and Lily rocketed downstream.

"Lily," Avery said. "Can you hear me?"

The little girl nodded. Storm swam alongside them, circled around, returned.

"I need you to grab on to the dog's neck. Can you do that?"

Avery held her breath, waiting. The instant Lily reached for the big K-9, Avery hefted her onto his back.

Storm immediately swam for the shore.

Avery tried to keep pace. Her arms and legs ached from battling the current. Still, her gaze stayed on her daughter as Storm scrambled out of the water with her.

Relief sent a wave of nausea rushing through her. The adrenaline subsided, sapping the last of her strength. She started to go under.

"Storm, guard!" Tristan yelled.

Was his the last voice she'd hear? A sense of peace settled over her. If nothing else, she'd managed to save Lily. And Tristan would see her safe.

Deena Alexander grew up in a small town on the south shore of eastern Long Island, where she met and married her high school sweetheart. She recently relocated to Florida with her husband, three kids, son-in-law and four dogs. Now she enjoys long walks in nature all year long, despite the occasional alligator or snake she sometimes encounters. Deena's love for writing developed when her youngest son was born and didn't sleep through the night.

Books by Deena Alexander

Love Inspired Suspense

Crime Scene Connection
Shielding the Tiny Target
Kidnapped in the Woods
Christmas in the Crosshairs
Hunted for the Holidays
Hiding the Witness
Exposing Lethal Secrets
Missing at Christmas

Missing Person Investigations

Seeking the Kidnapped Child

Visit the Author Profile page at LoveInspired.com.

SEEKING THE KIDNAPPED CHILD

DEENA ALEXANDER

LOVE INSPIRED SUSPENSE
INSPIRATIONAL ROMANCE

MIX
Paper | Supporting responsible forestry
FSC® C021394
www.fsc.org

LOVE INSPIRED® SUSPENSE
INSPIRATIONAL ROMANCE

Recycling programs for this product may not exist in your area.

ISBN-13: 978-1-335-91907-6

Seeking the Kidnapped Child

For questions and comments about the quality of this book, please contact us at CustomerService@Harlequin.com.

Love Inspired
22 Adelaide St. West, 41st Floor
Toronto, Ontario M5H 4E3, Canada
www.LoveInspired.com

HarperCollins Publishers
Macken House, 39/40 Mayor Street Upper,
Dublin 1, D01 C9W8, Ireland
www.HarperCollins.com

Printed in Lithuania

1 2 3 4 5 6 7 8 9 10 LIT 28 27 26 25

Come unto me, all ye that labour and
are heavy laden, and I will give you rest.
—*Matthew* 11:28

This book is lovingly dedicated to my daughter, Elaina.
Thank you so much for your support, encouragement
and help. I love you with all of my heart,
and I'm so proud of the woman you've become!

ONE

Avery Taylor clutched her sleeping daughter tighter, her fight-or-flight instincts begging her to do anything other than stand there, frozen, staring down the two masked gunmen blocking her from entering her home. "Please, I..."

But what could she say? Had she stumbled upon a home invasion? She couldn't imagine having anything either of them could possibly want. She lived off the beaten path. The small but cozy two-story bungalow she'd inherited from her grandfather sat alone on a cul-de-sac at the end of a long, winding mountain road. And she worked from home as a medical transcriptionist, supplementing her income with her inheritance to make ends meet. Well, whatever they wanted, they could have it, as long as they left her and her four-year-old, Liliana, alone. She opened her mouth to say as much.

The taller of the two lifted his weapon, his hand rock steady.

She could only assume he'd done this before.

"Where's Tristan McAvoy?" he demanded.

Her mouth snapped right back closed again. Once she recovered enough to try to answer, her voice shook before she could utter more than a grunt, and she worked to steady it. Although she didn't know why she bothered. It was clear she was terrified, and even more so now that she knew what they wanted…because she couldn't give it to them. "I don't know where Tristan is. I haven't seen him in almost five years."

Since he'd walked out on her and never looked back, despite her numerous attempts to get in touch with him and tell him he was going to be a father. He'd been her best friend, her love, her future, and then he'd been gone.

Her arms began to tremble beneath Liliana's weight, and Avery hefted her up higher so the little girl's head rested more comfortably on her shoulder. The last thing she needed was Lily waking to this mess. They'd attended a church festival that evening, and her daughter had passed out on the way home. It was a good thing Lily was a heavy sleeper.

The shorter man, who outweighed her by a good hundred pounds of pure muscle, gestured toward the front door with his weapon. "Get inside."

She hesitated.

"Look, Avery…"

The fact that he knew her name and had associated her with Tristan sent a chill racing up her spine, despite the heat of the summer night. If they knew all that, she had to figure they knew Lily was Tristan's daughter as well, even if Tristan didn't know. But how had they found out? True, she'd listed him as Lily's father on her birth certificate, but why would this stranger have access to that?

"All you have to do is tell us where to find McAvoy." The man's easy shrug belied the tension in his posture. "Once we have him, we'll let you and his kid go. Easy enough?"

It would be if she believed him, and if she had any

clue where to find Tristan, but she wasn't buying it. Then again, they did have on ski masks, which gave her some hope that they planned to let her go. If not, they'd have no reason to conceal their identities. Of course, she couldn't give them what they wanted. If she knew how to get ahold of Tristan, he'd know about his daughter.

An image of him flashed in her mind—his shaggy brown hair that just brushed his collar and always seemed in need of a trim, a smile that could melt her heart in an instant, his brilliant blue eyes that used to cage hers and fill her with hope for their future together. A hope that died when he walked away with promises to return once he'd gotten his head on straight. An empty promise, as it turned out.

She'd wanted to talk to him after he'd left, to tell him he was going to be a dad instead of imparting the news via voicemail, email or text. She'd wanted to gauge his reaction, so she'd simply asked him to call her back. Time and time again. And he hadn't. Not once. So, he'd never learned about his daughter. But that wasn't really fair. He'd left after his parents had been murdered, bitter and grief-stricken and so filled with anger she hadn't known what to do for him. Still, he could have answered at least one of her messages.

Focus, Avery.

She weighed her options. She could make a run for the car, where she'd left the doors standing open and her bags inside in hopes of retrieving them after she'd gotten Lily into bed, but she'd never outrun a bullet if these men intended to shoot her. Then again, they couldn't get information from her if she was dead. But they could incapacitate her. How could she risk leaving Liliana alone with these monsters? She couldn't. Which left her no choice but to do as they'd instructed.

Lily's weight was becoming a strain on her back and shoulders, and she didn't want to set her down on the stone walkway and risk waking her. But she did have to put her down. If it came down to it, she couldn't fight with Liliana in her arms. What did it matter if she went inside with them anyway? It wasn't like there was any chance of someone driving past to notice what was happening or being close enough to hear her screams. The secluded home she'd grown up in, that she'd always viewed as so peaceful and serene, a safe haven tucked against the side of the mountain, surrounded by fields and wildflowers, now seemed nothing but isolated. She'd never felt so frightened and alone, even after Tristan had left and her grandfather had passed away.

But if she could get inside, if she could get to her grandfather's hunting rifle hanging above the mantel, maybe she'd stand a chance of defending herself and her daughter.

Hoping to appear meek and docile, she kept her gaze averted as she said, "Let me get my daughter inside."

She sidestepped the shorter man and shoved the key into the lock, then pushed the front door open and stepped inside. The air-conditioning in the small entryway chilled the sweat that snaked down her hairline and along her back. Keeping track of the men flanking her in her peripheral vision, Avery prayed Liliana would remain asleep as she crossed the room, eyed the rifle hanging over the massive stone fireplace and climbed the stairs to Lily's bedroom. She set her daughter gently into bed then smoothed long, wispy strands of blond hair off her baby's face.

"God, please keep her safe," she whispered as she

tucked Lily's security blanket into her arms. *And help me get her out of this mess.*

Her back ached from standing still with Liliana's weight in her arms, and she pressed a hand against it.

"Hands where I can see them!"

She shot her hands in the air. As if she had a weapon stashed beneath her sundress. "I was just rubbing my back."

"Get downstairs!" He waved the weapon toward the stairway.

Anxious to get the gunman away from Lily, she followed him back to the living room.

"Sit down! Now!" He gestured toward a green-and-cream-patterned armchair that had been part of the bungalow's decor for as long as she could remember. "And don't try anything."

She perched on the edge of the seat cushion, prepared to attack given even the slightest opportunity.

The two men huddled together between the seating arrangement and the fireplace, their frantic murmurs too muffled for her to make out.

Ignoring them, she scanned the area. There was no way she'd make it across the room to the gun before they could reach her. Even if they didn't want to shoot her, they could easily overtake her.

The fireplace tools were also out of reach. As were the knives in the kitchen and anything else a rambunctious four-year-old could get into or hurt herself with.

Finally, the taller man pulled a phone from his pocket and scrolled as he walked out the front door, leaving the short, stocky guy staring at her.

He dropped onto the ottoman almost knee to knee with Avery, elbows resting on his knees, handgun clutched loosely. "Look, Avery, let's be realistic about this. I'm sure you've figured out by now there's no way out of this."

There's always a way out, she reminded herself, if only she could find it.

"All you have to do is tell us where to find McAvoy and we'll go." He spread his hands wide, as if his argument was perfectly rational, which it might have been if he wasn't holding her at gunpoint while he laid it out. "There's no reason for any harm to come to you or that pretty little girl of yours."

Her stomach heaved, turned over and threatened to rebel.

"Just tell me where to find McAvoy and I'll be on my way."

She started to ask him what this was about, hoping to at least stall him, but decided against the idea. She had a feeling the less she knew, the better off she'd be. She didn't bother trying to hide her tears, simply let them roll down her cheeks without swiping them away. The pain of her past combined with her current terror gripped her heart and squeezed. "I've been trying to tell you. I don't know where Tristan is. He walked out on me almost five years ago, after someone murdered his parents. I never spoke to him again after that."

Could this have anything to do with his parents' deaths? He'd insisted before he left that he didn't invite her to go with him because he wouldn't put her in the position of having to make a choice between him and her grandfather. He knew her grandfather's health was deteriorating and she wouldn't want to leave him, which was true, but she'd always suspected there was more to it. She'd often wondered, in the middle of the night, when the world was quiet and still, if he'd left to try to avenge his parents' deaths. As far as she knew, their attackers had never been found, and in their small mountain town, muggings and homicides were far from routine.

Had he finally hunted down their killers? Had he done something to them? He'd been so angry when he'd left, so determined to find justice. Maybe these men were seeking revenge for something Tristan had done.

Either way, it didn't matter right now. At the moment, all that mattered was getting these men out of her house and calling the police. "I've tried to get in touch with him to tell him about his daughter, but he never responded to any of my attempts. I honestly have no idea how to find him."

Her voice shook, but there was nothing she could do about that.

"Well, then..." The guy straightened, stared her down.

If she managed to survive this, she'd remember those ice-cold eyes for the rest of her life. Given the opportunity, she'd be able to identify him.

He shoved to his feet, aimed the weapon at her head. "I guess we'll do this the hard way."

Avery held her hands up in front of her. As if they could ward off bullets. "Please. I don't know what I can tell you. I don't have the information you're looking for."

"If you don't know where McAvoy is, I suggest you find him." Spittle sprayed. He started to pace, pressing the heel of his gun hand against his forehead and muttering something incoherent.

Whatever he wanted with Tristan, it couldn't be good. Would she give him the information if she had it? She'd probably say or do anything to get this man out of her house and away from her daughter. She could always try again to contact Tristan and warn him he might be in danger once the man was gone. If the guy didn't kill her first.

"I've tried to find him, numerous times. I don't know how." She sobbed softly, giving up any hope of controlling her emotions.

He stopped in front of her, contemplated her, then kicked her chair. "Get a pen and paper."

Reeling, she frowned at him. "For what?"

He grabbed her long, blond ponytail and yanked her to her feet, then shoved her toward a desk in the corner. "So you can remember what you're supposed to do when you come to."

"Come to?" What was he talking about?

"I am fast running out of patience." He pressed the muzzle hard against her temple. "Get the pen and paper. Now."

She nodded, the cold metal moving with her, then crossed the room and grabbed a pad and pen from her desk drawer. She turned to face him. "Okay."

He pulled the desk chair out and shoved her into it. "Start writing."

Her hands shook wildly as she uncapped the pen and held it poised over the pad.

"You track down Tristan McAvoy."

She started to turn toward him, to plead with him. "But I—"

He backhanded her hard across the face, the sting of the slap a stark reminder of what was at stake. "I don't care how you do it. You find him. And you tell him he is not to testify at the upcoming trial."

Her heart pounded hard enough to rock her back and forth, bringing a wave of motion sickness. She wrote exactly what he said, word for word, though the letters were barely legible, her hands were shaking so badly. “What trial?”

“He’ll know.”

She nodded, sniffed. “Okay. Anything else?”

“Yeah, do not contact the police.”

“Okay.” Though that was exactly what she planned to do the instant they walked out of her house. Maybe the police could track down Tristan and pass along the message.

“As long as you follow our instructions to the letter, and Tristan comes out of hiding, your daughter will be returned to—”

“No!” Terror seized her. She lurched to her feet, tumbling the chair to the side.

He ignored the outburst. “Liliana will be returned unharmed.”

“Please. Leave Liliana alone. I’ll do anything you ask. There’s no reason to take her.” *Oh, God, please don’t let them take my little girl.* “Please.”

“You have one week to find McAvoy and stop him from testifying.” He aimed the handgun at her, then a slow smile spread through the hole in his mask. He shifted the weapon slowly toward the stairway. “If you make any attempt to notify law enforcement or contact anyone other than McAvoy, we will know, and we will dispose of his daughter.”

Rage surged through her. She bent and grabbed the chair back, barely hefted the would-be weapon and swung as hard as she could.

The chair slammed into the man’s shoulder and broke apart. The gun flew from his hand. Before Avery could scramble after the weapon, he staggered for an instant, then regained his footing and lunged for her.

A well-aimed kick to the groin slowed him down. She

raked his cheek with her nails, wishing they were longer, but at least she'd have his DNA beneath them if he killed her. Which was what he'd have to do if he wanted to take her baby out of this house.

He shoved her back.

She landed hard on the floor, slammed her elbow and saw stars, then rolled and jumped back to her feet, knees bent, braced to fight.

Something cold and hard hit her temple.

She lurched to the side, staggered, bent at the waist, sucking in air, desperate to hold on to consciousness.

The guy's partner stood over her, gun raised high. Then he brought the weapon down again.

Her knees buckled. Blackness encroached, tunneling her vision as the other guy ran up the stairs then returned with Liliana flung carelessly over his shoulder.

Avery tried to cry out, to gain her footing, to reach her child.

Lily, awake and screaming, pummeled the man's back with her tiny fists. "Mama!"

The last thing Avery saw as the shorter man walked out was her little girl's frightened expression, before his partner hit her again and she went down and lost her battle with unconsciousness.

Memories tormented Tristan McAvoy as he barreled up the winding mountain road toward the house where Avery had always lived—not the horrible memories of pain and grief he'd expected and prepared himself for—but sweet memories of a time when he'd still been innocent and naive. If possible, those memories were even more painful. He eased off the accelerator as he rounded a hairpin curve. It wouldn't do Avery any good if he got himself killed before he could get to her.

Avery Taylor. Talk about torturous memories. If he closed his eyes, which he didn't dare do as he wound his way up the mountain, he could still feel her fingers entwined with his as they hiked the familiar trails behind her grandfather's home. He could see her long, dark blond hair rippling on the soft breeze, the sun's rays catching all the lighter blond and strawberry highlights, and her killer smile as she'd pointed out any wildlife they happened upon. She'd been the love of his life, his everything, his entire world—until the day that had changed his life forever.

But getting lost in the void of the past wouldn't help him now. He glanced over his shoulder to be sure Storm, his K-9 partner, was still lying comfortably on the back seat of the rental car. He'd prefer the big Newfoundland to be in a carrier, but there hadn't been time to procure a properly outfitted department-issued vehicle to secure the 140-pound FBI search-and-rescue dog before the chopper had reached Timberwood Falls. Storm was trained to ride in many different types of vehicles, under a variety of circumstances, so he'd be fine. Tristan still worried, though. After all, Storm was the only companion Tristan hadn't shut out after losing his good friend a year ago, the only being he had to worry about. At least, he had been until last night.

He shifted, sat up straighter, needing to pay attention if he was going to make it to Avery in time to save her daughter—*his* daughter. His heart hitched. He had a daughter. He still couldn't wrap his head around that fact, couldn't process the emotions coursing through him—love for both the Avery he'd known and the child he'd yet to meet, joy at the thrill of realizing he wasn't as alone in the world as he'd thought, regret at the time he'd wasted running away from a past he hadn't had the courage to confront, followed almost instantly by stark terror and guilt.

The shock of hearing from Avery after all these years, and the news of his little girl, had come as a blow, and he'd barely had time to register or react to it before learning that Avery and the child were both in danger. Because of him.

Although he'd never returned any of her past calls, he'd listened to all her messages, often wondering what his life might have been like if he hadn't decided to make a clean break. But that didn't matter now. He'd left. And she'd stopped trying to reach him a long time ago. For a moment, when he'd first seen her number on his missed calls list the day before, his heart had soared at the opportunity to hear her voice again. But her message, filled with frantic pleas to come save their daughter, had knocked him for a loop.

So he did what he'd always done: stuffed all those mixed feelings into a tidy little box, closed the lid and tucked it away in a corner of his heart where it couldn't affect him. At least, that's what he told himself. And then he did what he should have done five years ago. He responded to her call.

He didn't know much about the little girl, only what Avery's hysterical, rambling message had conveyed. The child had been abducted. Her kidnappers demanded that Tristan refuse to testify at the upcoming illegal-adoption trial he'd spent the past three years preparing for if Avery ever hoped to see her girl again. Of course, Tristan wasn't naive enough to believe her captors would ever let the child go. He knew they'd eliminate all witnesses, including Avery and her daughter, the instant they no longer needed them to hold over Tristan's head. Well, no way was he going to let that happen.

When he'd fled Timberwood Falls for the East Coast, he'd vowed never to return. But when he'd been offered a position with the FBI in Montana, a promotion to the kind of team he'd worked so hard to join, he'd been unable to refuse the move back to his home state. And he'd assured himself the chances of catching a case in the small, barely-a-dot-on-the-map town he'd grown up in were slim to none. So, he'd simply steered clear. And yet look where he'd ended up. He shifted uncomfortably in his seat.

Of every agent in the FBI's Montana Missing Persons Unit, he'd been chosen to lead the mission into the black-market adoption ring for a reason. In addition to his skills, training and seniority, he had no ties, no family to be threatened. The families of all the other task force members had been given protection, because the higher-up members of the adoption ring they'd taken down probably commanded more resources than his own unit did. And because the crime boss Gianna Rossi had escaped. Tristan had left his family out on their own, to fend for themselves, because he hadn't even bothered to learn they existed. He'd thought, when his parents died five years ago, that his only living family was gone.

He rubbed the exhaustion from his eyes. For now, it was enough to know the child was in immediate danger. Everything else could come later. When anger toward Avery tried to surface, he shoved it back down. He'd received her messages pleading with him to call her back during the months after he'd first left, and he'd chosen to ignore them. He knew he couldn't return to her, understood she wouldn't leave her ailing grandfather to follow him, and he'd assured himself he was doing her a favor by making a clean break. Too bad he didn't realize sooner he was more concerned with making the breakup easier on himself.

Of course, she could have told him in any one of the messages that he was going to be a father. Would it have changed things? Who knew? But at least he'd have had the chance to decide. He tried again to shake off the roller coaster of emotions. They wouldn't do him, Avery or their little girl a bit of good. If anything, they'd hinder his ability to do his job.

A quick glance at the dashboard clock told him he only had a few hours left to meet the deadline Avery had imposed. Twenty-four hours, that was all she'd said she'd wait before going to the police to report Liliana missing. *Liliana.* The fact that she'd named her little girl, their little girl, after his mother brought an ache to his heart so bad it was a wonder it didn't simply give out under the strain. Avery had obviously still been thinking of him as she'd gone through her pregnancy alone, given birth alone, gone home with their child alone.

How could she ever forgive him for abandoning her? How could he ever forgive himself? That was one answer he did have—he couldn't.

Rounding the last curve yanked his attention back to the matter at hand. He might not ever be able to make up for the past, but he would save Avery's child in the present. He would ease the pain and sheer terror filling her voice in the message she'd left him. That was the least he could do after he'd ignored all her other attempts to reach him. He'd read every text and email and listened to every voicemail back then. Even the terse *call me*'s after she'd gone from pleading to cajoling to straight-out anger were enough to elicit a reaction from him, a longing to smooth her hair back, to see her smile, to hear her laugh. He'd thought about reaching out to her over the years, but as time went on, it became more and more difficult to face her. It had been easier to make a clean break. So, aside from the twice-yearly phone calls to the sheriff in charge of his parents' case, which had yet to net him any new information, he'd left Timberwood Falls behind and ignored the one woman who might have been able to lure him back.

He didn't dare let his thoughts wander toward Sheriff Reynolds or his lack of progress in solving his parents' case—one of the only murders ever to occur in town. The anger that welled up at the thought would only hinder is ability to focus.

He slowed even more, scanning the field surrounding the bungalow, searching deeper into the shadows of the woods bordering the property. Although the massive pines packed thickly together along the perimeter would make it impossible for him to know if anyone was hiding among the shadows. He hadn't called ahead, worried his enemies might intercept the call. The Rossi network was vast, even after the FBI had corralled a good portion of it, and he had no doubt they'd already set up surveillance in anticipation of his arrival. His only hope was to get in, grab Avery and get out as quickly as possible. *If* she'd even go with him.

He and his team had discussed sending another agent to pick her up, but the people who'd abducted Liliana would consider that a betrayal. If they saw any other law enforcement officers, or even a close friend, show up at the house, they'd most likely just kill everyone and search for another way to get to Tristan.

It was clear to Tristan that they had abducted the girl not to threaten him but to draw him out. Once he was in the enemy's sights, they'd kill him, silencing him for good. Then eliminate any other witnesses. A lump lodged in his throat. He needed to get Avery out—carefully. Then they had to find Liliana. He could only hope Avery would have known not to call anyone else. She'd said she wouldn't in her message, but sitting alone for twenty-plus hours while your child was missing would be nearly impossible for anyone, even someone who might have trusted him, which Avery had absolutely no reason to do. Then again, she was probably used to dealing with things alone, thanks to him.

For the first time since his parents' funeral, he uttered a prayer. "Please, God, don't let any harm come to Avery or Liliana. I know I turned away from You in anger and despair. I know I've done enough terrible things to earn Your wrath, but please don't take that out on them. I've already hurt them enough."

Then another thought intruded, threatening his focus: What if Avery wasn't alone? What if she'd married and another man was raising his child? He dismissed the discomfort that came with the thought. Avery deserved happiness, and it wasn't like he'd ever returned a single call to her. Whatever the case, he'd have to suck it up, deal with it like a professional and make sure everyone got out safe.

He scanned the immediate area as he pulled onto the lawn, turned around and stopped the sedan parallel to the front door so they could make a quick escape. He shifted into Park. "Storm, down. Stay."

Fully confident the big dog would obey the commands, he left the car running and the driver's side door open, yanked the back driver's side door open and ran the few feet to the front door.

Without warning, the door swung inward, and there she stood. Avery's jade eyes, once so trusting and innocent, held the kind of intense fear that only came with learning what a tough place the world could be.

And he loathed himself for being the cause of that fear. But he couldn't leave her exposed. Blocking her as best he could, he hooked her arm and guided her inside even as he slammed the door shut behind him.

"Tristan, please—" With that, she collapsed into sobs.

He caught her, held her in his arms as she cried against his chest. He inhaled deeply, the familiar scent of her shampoo almost his undoing. And he wished he could keep her in his embrace forever, cocoon her in safety, turn back time and stay with her—do anything other than walk away from her then and push her away now. "I'm so sorry, Avery. I didn't know. If I did, I—"

He what? Would have come sooner? Would have seen to it they were protected? His assurances would mean nothing to her, especially when he didn't even know the truth himself.

Avery shoved him back, swiped the heels of her hands over her blotchy cheeks and red-rimmed eyes. Then she balled her fists and pounded against his chest, over and over again, demanding answers. "What is going on, Tristan? Why would anyone take Lily? You have to get my baby back!"

He gripped her arms and set her back, not to stop her from beating on him, but because there simply was no time. "Avery, listen to me. I have no right to ask anything of you, but I need you to trust me."

"Trust you?" She snorted, not that he could blame her,

then grabbed a worn pink-and-cream baby blanket from the back of the sectional and hugged it tightly against her. Blood had dried on her temple, in more than one spot, but it didn't seem as if she'd administered any kind of first aid. They'd have to get a doctor to deal with it later. As long as she could move, it was more important to get out of there and find somewhere safe to hole up, get medical treatment and make a plan.

"We're going to get Liliana back. I promise you that." Though years in law enforcement had taught him it was a promise he couldn't make and might very well not be able to keep. "But I have to get you out of here first. Right now. The longer we wait the more danger we're in—"

"I don't care about you or me or us. I only care about getting my little girl back safely."

The dismissal cut deep. Seriously, though, what had he expected, a warm, open-armed welcome? Yeah, right. "I understand. But I need you to listen to me. I'll explain everything to you once we're gone."

He yanked the curtains closed over the front window to keep anyone from seeing inside. He wrapped one hand around the doorknob and gripped her elbow with the other. "I need you to go straight out—"

She ripped her arm out of his grasp. "I'm not going anywhere with you until you tell me what's going on and how you plan to get my daughter back. I've already waited almost a full day when the police should already have been notified and there should already have been an Amber Alert issued so everyone would be looking for her. I won't wait another minute."

"Avery, please. The longer we stand here arguing, the less chance we'll be able to get Liliana back." The name brought a pang of grief he had no choice but to ignore. The fate of the woman she'd been named for would not be this child's fate. "I assure you, people are already searching for her. Just come with me. Let me get you to my team, explain what's going on and then, if you still want to go to the police, I'll take you there myself."

She eyed him with suspicion, tremors coursing through her, but at least she didn't argue further.

Taking that as acquiescence, he parted the curtains a fraction of an inch and peered out the front window, then unholstered his weapon. "They will probably expect me to remain here more than a few minutes, so we have to move now, right away. I want you to keep your head low, go straight to the car parked in front of the door and slide into the back seat. Do not hesitate for an instant, no matter what happens, and don't be frightened by the dog in the back. That's Storm, my K-9 partner, and he won't hurt you. Do you understand?"

She nodded, sniffed and clutched the blanket closer.

"Once you're in the car, keep your head down as low as possible." Without waiting for her to argue or ask questions, he yanked the front door open and propelled her through it, then hunched over right on her heels with his weapon held ready.

Gunfire erupted almost immediately from the tree line, shattering the sedan's windows as well as those along the front of the house.

Avery let out a small squeal and covered her head with one arm and held the blanket against her with the other as she ducked low and ran, exactly as he'd instructed. The instant she dived into the back seat, he slammed the door shut behind her and jumped into the driver's seat. He stomped on the gas pedal, fishtailing even as he swung the door shut.

He slouched in the seat, making himself as small a target as possible, and didn't bother returning fire. This was not a fight he could win. Instead, his only goal was to get Avery, Storm and himself out of there alive. He'd have plenty of time to return for his attackers after he saw Avery safe and found Liliana.

"Did you know they'd start shooting?" she yelled.

"I expected they would." The back end skidded as he left the patchy lawn and hit the dirt driveway. He recovered quickly and rocketed onto the single-lane road that would lead them down the mountain. The gunfire stopped. Silence descended. "Get a seat belt on and keep your head down."

Before she could follow his instructions, a loud roar followed by a dull rumble split the silence. "Wait!"

The rocket-propelled grenade hit the back window and went straight through and out the front windshield. If they fired one… He slammed the brakes. "Dive out and roll! Into the woods. Now! Go!"

Without waiting for him to say anything else, she flung the door open and jumped.

"Storm, out!"

The big dog followed her instantly.

Even as the sound of the next RPG descended on him, Tristan threw his door open and rolled off the side of the road and into the woods.

This time the RPG found its mark, probably the gas tank. An explosion tore through the car, and it burst into flames. Heat enveloped him, singeing the hair on his arms as he flung them over his head and continued to roll. Brush and twigs clawed at him, and he crashed to a stop hard against a tree, knocking the breath from his lungs. Hopefully, by not slowing the car, he'd bought them a few minutes to escape before their attackers realized they hadn't been inside the vehicle when it went up. But they didn't have time to wait. They had to move. Now. Because the men who'd opened fire would be coming as soon as they realized they hadn't finished the job they'd started.

TWO

Brambles tugged at Avery's hair, scratched her face and arms, and caught on the jeans and T-shirt she'd changed into after Lily was taken. She hugged her daughter's blanket closer as she rolled into the woods, clinging to it like a lifeline between her and her child. Once she cleared the tree line and felt reasonably concealed, she lay on her back, staring up at the towering pines and small patches of blue sky peeking through, and tried to get her bearings. Pain radiated through her head, tunneling her vision. Had she reinjured herself? Or was it the stress of the situation? Who knew? All she knew was…

She had to find Lily. She had to move. They were in danger. Where was Tristan? Had he escaped the explosion? Was he injured—or worse? And what about Storm? Fear clutched her throat, squeezed, threatened to choke her. She couldn't lie there all night. She had to get to Tristan and Storm, see if they needed help. Shadows had already begun to deepen along the mountain. Darkness would follow soon enough, and it would be more difficult to navigate the hazardous terrain. Especially with killers on their trail. And these were the same monsters that had her daughter.

Her breathing hitched. Falling apart wouldn't help.

She pressed the soft blanket against her face and inhaled deeply. The scents of baby shampoo and something uniquely Lily that still clung to the security blanket her little girl always slept with helped to calm her, allowed her to regain her focus. She rolled onto her side, started to call out for Tristan and Storm, then thought better of the idea. No sense alerting their attackers to their position if they hadn't already figured it out.

She sat up, waited a minute for the soft breeze rippling through the shrubbery to help clear her head, then looked around. A wave of relief washed over her when she spotted Storm on his feet, seemingly unharmed. Then she realized he was bent over, nudging at something in the bushes at the base of a tree with his nose.

Tristan!

Don't you dare leave me again, Tristan. Not while Lily is in danger and needs your help. Was that her only concern? That Lily needed him? Did Avery need him, too? For what? Comfort? No. She needed him to find Lily, nothing more. Tristan McAvoy had nothing else to offer her. Except, maybe, once Lily was home safe in her arms, the truth about why he'd left. Had he ever loved her? Or had their entire relationship—his promises of marriage, a family, a home, his assurances that they'd stand together through thick and thin forever—been a lie? One she'd fallen for hook, line and sinker. Well, she was no longer that same gullible, naive young woman. She'd learned the difference between fantasy and reality five years ago. Still, she couldn't leave him to die in the woods.

She pressed her hand against a thick tree trunk and used it to help her regain her footing, then stood, swaying, and gently prodded her temple with her fingertips. They came away bloody. Nothing she could do about that now. She wiped the blood on her jeans, careful not to stain Lily's blanket. Her daughter would need it more than ever when they found her. She moved forward, one step at a time, slowly scanning her surroundings so as not to set off a wave of dizziness.

She wiped the tears blurring her vision—they wouldn't do her any good—and stepped over a fallen log, careful to watch for rattlesnakes that might be camouflaged amid the carpet of dead leaves. It would be easy to miss them in the fading sunlight. Brittle leaves and twigs crunched beneath her feet with each step. She paused, flared her senses, listening for any disruption in the sounds of nature. Nothing. The men must not have reached the car yet, assuming they'd stop to check the car for their bodies before searching the woods. She resumed her trek, increasing her speed as she gained her footing and her confidence. They were nowhere near far enough from the road, and she had to get to Tristan and get out of there before their attackers caught up.

She'd forgiven Tristan after she'd found faith while she was pregnant, alone and terrified. But forgiveness wasn't trust. And, while she might have faith he'd do his best to get her out of this mess alive and find Lily, she didn't trust him with her heart. She wouldn't. She couldn't. She'd never trust anyone again. It seemed every time she did, every time she opened her heart and allowed herself to love someone, they left her.

Her parents had abandoned her when she was only three years old, had left her with her grandfather and gone off to see the world they'd missed out on after having her when they were in their late teens. Then they'd died in a car crash in some foreign country a few years later and never returned to her. Would they have? Eventually? If they hadn't been taken? She had no idea. But she doubted it. Just like she knew in her heart Tristan would never have come back if not for the situation with Lily.

Then, Liliana, Tristan's mother, who'd taken Avery under her wing and become the mother figure she'd longed for, had been violently taken from her. As Avery had lain in the hospital bed, clutching her newborn daughter in her arms, envisioning the way her birth should have gone, surrounded by Tristan, his parents and her grandfather, the ache had become unbearable. And she'd named her daughter for the woman she'd loved and grieved like her own mother. Five years had done nothing to dull the pain in her heart. She couldn't begin to imagine the agony Tristan must have suffered.

And now, even her grandfather, who'd been bedridden since Lily was born, was gone. He'd held on for so long, had fought so hard to stay with her, but he'd lost his battle with cancer last year. Despite his best efforts, and his incredible love for both her and Lily, he'd been taken, too. He'd have stayed with her if he could have. She clung to that.

Her heart ached unbearably, grief threatening to overwhelm her. Did Lily feel the same sense of abandonment Avery had felt growing up? Did she think she was alone in the world? How frightened must she be? Did she cling to hope that her mother would return for her, or had she given up? Avery wouldn't leave her daughter for anything. A sob she had no hope of stifling burst out, and she slapped a hand over her mouth to keep from drawing attention. She had to get a grip, or she would die there on the side of that mountain before she could find Lily. No way would she let that happen.

With a renewed sense of determination, Avery reached

Storm and laid a hand on his head. Brambles clung to his thick, black coat. She kept her voice a whisper, hoping he'd hear her and understand. "It's okay, boy."

He looked up at her through soulful eyes, then whimpered once.

Tristan stared up at her from where he lay tangled amid the brambles. He seemed to be struggling to breathe as he worked his way out of the mess.

She dropped to her knees, keeping low. "Are you okay?"

He nodded and sucked in a shallow breath. "Just… knocked…the wind…"

"Do you think you can get out of there?"

He nodded again and continued to disentangle himself from the thorny branches, then clutched his ribs and hissed through his teeth as he tried to stand.

Avery hooked him beneath one arm and helped him to his feet.

He leaned a shoulder against a nearby tree, took a few deep breaths, then pulled a phone from his jeans pocket. He gripped her chin between a thumb and forefinger and tipped her head to the side, studying the wound on her temple. "You all right to move?"

"Yes." She'd crawl off this mountain if that's what it took to reach her daughter.

"Okay." He looked around then pulled out his phone and dialed. "Give me one minute."

She nodded and reached up without thinking to brush a few stray leaves from his thick brown hair. But then she stopped. He wore it different now. Back when they'd been together, he'd kept it longer, so it just brushed his collar, and he was always shoving it out of his face. Though the top was still shaggy, the sides were cut short now.

When he reached up absently and raked a hand through the strands, she turned away. She'd do well to remember this wasn't the same boy she'd known.

She stepped back, sucked in a deep, steadying breath, then choked on thick, cloying smoke. How had she not noticed the column billowing from the car fire? The whole forest would go up if they couldn't extinguish it. She started forward, though she had no idea what she'd use to douse the flames. The hoses she kept hanging on each side of her house wouldn't reach that far down the road. But she had to at least warn the others that lived in the isolated area. And she had to soak her house and the land immediately surrounding it.

Tristan reached out and gently took her arm.

When she glanced back at him, he released her and held up a finger for her to wait before returning his attention to his call.

"Move in. We have a car fire, which, between the wind and dry conditions, will spread quickly." He spoke so softly she wasn't sure whoever was on the other end of the line could even hear him, but a muffled response she couldn't make out came almost instantly. "Yeah, I've acquired her, and we're moving out."

Acquired her? What was she, an item? Property? A target? Then she took notice of how banged up he was, cuts marring his face, bruises already blooming on his arms. He stood bent slightly to the side, one arm still wrapped around his middle, cradling his ribs. And she softened as she waited for him to stuff the phone back into his pocket.

He pushed away from the tree, winced and gasped a quick breath, then seemed to shake off whatever pain he might be in and leaned close to her. "We can't stay here."

She glanced around, more than ready to get out of

there, though the throbbing in her head begged her to sit down and close her eyes for even just a few minutes. "Which way?"

"Storm, heel." He issued the command softly as he pointed uphill and started walking, his hand resting companionably on the big dog's head as he trotted along at his side.

She fell into step beside him even as she second-guessed his decision. "But the fire will most likely start to spread this way."

"I know, but once the men who attacked us get to the car and realize we're not in it, they'll try to figure out which way we went and track us." He paused for a moment and looked over his shoulder. "They'll expect us to head down the mountain, since that makes the most sense."

"So, you think we can get away from them if we head up?"

"No." His piercing cobalt eyes turned somber as he met her gaze, the stark honesty she found there disarming. "They'll definitely find us. They are well equipped. I'm just trying to buy us as much time as I can until my team can reach us and get us out of here."

"How are they going to do that?"

He hesitated, then averted his gaze and started walking again. "We already had several extraction plans in place before I got here."

Avery fell silent as she tried to wrap her head around the fact that the man walking alongside her was the same guy she'd had a crush on throughout elementary school then dated all through high school and college, the guy she'd fallen in love with, the guy she'd sometimes allowed herself to remember in quiet moments over the years. Not that there weren't still similarities—there were. Every once in a while, she noticed a familiar gesture. His stride was still the same, no nonsense, eating up the yards as if he were on a mission. Which, she supposed, now he was.

He'd grown, filled out, hardened. He was no longer slim and gangly, but tall and muscular. Any sign of the playful, adventurous young man he'd been had disappeared, and she was surprised to find it saddened her. And yet, his eyes hadn't changed, and under different circumstances, she was afraid she could still lose herself in them.

But these weren't different circumstances, and they were no longer children. They'd grown apart, separated by time, distance and pain. And yet, he had come when she'd needed him most, had come to save her daughter—*their* daughter—when he didn't have to. Would he have come sooner, come right away, if she'd ever found the courage to tell him about his daughter? Had she been selfish—wanted him to return to her not only because of Lily but because he loved her? She'd thought about reaching out to him again over the years as she watched Lily grow. She should have. She realized that now. She'd been so caught up in feelings of abandonment, first by her parents and then by Tristan, that she hadn't thought clearly enough. Had she truly refrained from telling him about his daughter via message because she'd thought it best to tell him in person? Or had her fear of rejection kept her from telling him?

The silence between them grew uncomfortable, and she ached for some way to lessen the rift. If they were going to work together to find Lily, they would need to at least get along. The past was past. It didn't matter now. Only saving Lily did. "I'm sorry, Tristan."

"Sorry?" He narrowed his gaze on her. "Sorry for what?"

She swallowed hard, the thickening smoke burning her throat. "I was difficult when you first arrived. I apologize. I was desperate to find Lily, to get answers, and I never even thanked you for coming, and I should have. So, thank you."

But that was all she'd apologize for. The fact that she could have, maybe even should have, simply texted him that she was carrying his child burned in her chest, and she had no idea what to do with that. She'd been frightened and devastated that he'd left and never bothered to answer her after he'd promised to return.

"Avery…" Even though his throat worked, Adam's apple bobbing, he remained silent. Tears streamed from the corners of his eyes, leaving tracks through the dirt and blood on his cheeks.

She figured the smoke was getting to him as well. They would have to change direction soon if the flames continued to spread. She jumped, startled from her thoughts when he spoke again a few minutes later.

"You don't owe me an apology, or anything else." He stopped walking for a moment and turned to face her. "I'm the one who's sorry. I…"

She waited, but he simply shook his head.

"This isn't the time for this conversation. Right now, we need to concentrate on getting out of here."

"And finding Lily." Because, in the end, that was all that mattered to her.

Then he turned away and continued up the mountain, picking his way through brush, climbing over fallen logs and weaving between the thick pines.

"Where are we meeting your team?"

"Do you remember the old field up by the Jansen Ranch?"

Her heart hitched. She remembered it all too well, the times they'd ridden horses up there, spread a blanket amid the wildflowers and enjoyed a picnic lunch, then hopped from boulder to boulder down the stream. "But that's ten or twelve miles from here. It'll take hours for us to hike all the way there. We can't take that long, Tristan. Lily is alone somewhere with those monsters."

"We'll find her." He reached out but then let his hand fall to his side. "Even though we're here, my team is already searching, contacting informants and trying to find Lily. We're really good at what we do. We *will* find her."

She wanted so badly to believe him, to trust him, but she just couldn't find it in herself to do so. So, they hiked the mountain in silence. She didn't bother to look in the direction of the only home she'd ever known as they skirted her property at a distance. What did it matter anyway? Lily was what made it a home after her grandfather had passed away. It was all she could do to stay on her feet and keep plodding forward.

"One of the men who attacked me said you work for the FBI?" The guy she remembered had had dreams of being an architect.

"Yes. After my..." He hesitated. "After I left here, I went to work for the FBI, and now I'm part of a specialized missing persons unit."

She considered leaving it at that, figured she was better off not knowing too much, but what difference did it make how much she knew? They'd already tried to kill her once. "Is that why they don't want you to testify?"

He nodded. "I recently led an investigation into the disappearances of several children in Montana. It took us a while to figure out the cases were related, but once we did, I was tasked with coordinating the investigations and finding proof. And then I went in undercover."

"And did you? Find proof, I mean." Her legs trembled as she climbed over a downed tree with a little help from Tristan.

"Yes. A prominent attorney with vast resources at her disposal was the head of a black-market adoption ring… or, I guess, she still is. She managed to disappear when we took down a good portion of her organization. And she'll stop at nothing to keep her multibillion-dollar network up and running. Unfortunately, that means stopping me from testifying, since not only can I see to it that the thugs we've already apprehended go to prison for a very long time, but I'm the only one who can identify her as the leader and the only one willing, or left alive, to testify to the other atrocities I witnessed her commit." He paused, held up a hand for Avery to stop and frowned.

She did as he indicated, squashing a million questions begging for answers, and listened intently for any sounds of pursuit.

Storm growled low in his throat.

Tristan put a finger to his lips, and the dog quieted almost instantly, then he motioned both her and Storm to duck between a couple of thick hemlocks and pulled his weapon. He crouched beside them.

The last remnants of the sun set amid an orange glow that might well be coming from the spreading fire, and then darkness claimed the forest. Avery buried her face in Lily's blanket and inhaled deeply, held her breath and waited.

Tristan stayed low amid the hemlock tree's thick, drooping branches, his ears open for whatever sound he'd heard that had alerted him to another presence in the forest. He'd do well to remember gunmen weren't the only creatures roaming the forest or fleeing the fire. He worked to steady his breathing, easing shallow breaths in and out slowly, all too aware of the scent of blood emanating from both him and Avery.

Storm crouched beside him, perfectly still and silent, ready to defend. Although the big Newfie was specifically trained for water search and rescue, rather than as a guard dog, he'd still come to Tristan's defense if necessary.

Avery kept her face pressed to the baby blanket she'd taken from the house, the sounds of her ragged breathing muffled by the cloth. And it reminded him of an idea he'd had earlier, but it would have to wait until he'd dealt with whatever immediate danger might be approaching.

Silence surrounded him, but he wasn't fooled. Even if he had been gone for the past five years, he'd grown up in these woods, and he recognized the absolute stillness that warned of a predator on the hunt.

He remained perfectly motionless, willing himself to blend into his surroundings, and peered between the branches. It only took only a couple of minutes for a massive cougar to emerge from the cover of the forest into a very small clearing a few feet away from them. It stopped, lifted its head, twitched its nose. Even as it fled the thickening smoke and flames, the animal would stop to investigate the scent of blood, sensing a weaker animal to prey upon. They couldn't hide from him, and it wasn't likely he'd pass up the opportunity for an easy meal.

Tristan slid his weapon slowly back into its holster. He didn't want to kill the beautiful cat if he didn't have to. Nor did he want to draw the attention of his attackers, which a gunshot most certainly would. Then again, so would the sounds of a scuffle between him and the two-hundred-pound cougar.

The animal prowled closer to the hemlock trees, sniffing the air. It was mere feet away now, seconds away from discovering them. Flames encroached. They had to move. He gestured for Avery and Storm to stay put, then stepped out onto the narrow trail. If nothing else, he could draw the animal's attention and give Avery a chance to escape. Even if the thought of her fleeing alone up the mountainside with a rapidly spreading wildfire nipping at her heels and killers no doubt right behind her had his blood running cold.

The big cat went instantly still, a deadly predator facing its prey.

Tristan lifted his arms over his head and waved them back and forth in an effort to appear larger. He'd have to forgo making any loud noises for the moment. Careful to maintain eye contact with the animal, he took a step backward, then another. If he just backed away, maybe the cougar would move on.

The cat kept pace, stalking him, creeping forward with incredible grace and without making a sound.

Tristan didn't dare look away. His heart rate kicked up, breaths coming more rapidly between fear and the thickening smoke. Adrenaline surged through him. As he took another step back, he held one hand out to the side and motioned for Avery to move. Hopefully, she'd do so slowly and not draw the cougar's attention. If he could keep it occupied long enough, she could probably move far enough away to get off its radar. He lowered his hand to hover over his weapon. He needed Avery out of the way before he risked whatever a gunshot might attract.

The cougar stilled, stared him down, a dull roar rumbling in its chest. It lowered into a crouch, bunching its muscular legs beneath it, quivering as it readied to pounce.

Tristan backpedaled.

Instead of fleeing, Avery stepped out from behind the tree and positioned herself right next to him. She raised her arms high. Blood trickled down her hairline from her temple. The wind shifted. Smoke billowed into the clearing, enveloping the cougar, effectively camouflaging the dangerous animal, concealing it from view.

Flames devoured the dry brush, racing toward them.

They were going to have to run. He gestured to Avery. "Go!"

She eyed him for a moment, her gaze tortured, then turned and did as he'd said.

The cougar launched itself after her with lightning speed.

Tristan kicked out, landing a hard blow against the animal's side as it passed, knocking it off its feet. It rolled and easily regained its footing.

Storm jumped between Avery and the cougar, barking loudly.

"Storm, no!" But it was too late to preserve any hope of keeping the encounter silent.

Storm obeyed instantly, keeping his gaze locked on the cougar, who stood stunned for a moment, then splayed its legs and faced down both Tristan and the dog, who stood between it and its intended meal.

With the thickening smoke, he didn't dare risk firing his weapon and perhaps hitting another animal. Besides, there was no way to know for sure no hunters or campers would be nearby. Tristan lunged toward the big cat and yelled, no longer concerned about silence. They'd already made enough noise to alert anyone nearby to their presence.

The animal bounced back and forth on its front paws, its gaze riveted on Storm.

Automatic gunfire tore through the brush, shredding leaves and bushes.

The cougar whirled, skidded on the dry leaves, then took off in the opposite direction.

"Storm, down!" Tristan dived for cover. With the thick smoke, it was impossible to tell exactly where the shots had come from. And he'd lost track of Avery. He belly crawled in the direction he'd seen her running, keeping his head low. He put a finger to his lips to be sure the big dog remained quiet.

Storm followed the silent command, as he'd been trained to do, and crept alongside him.

"There's nowhere to go, McAvoy." The voice came from uphill, trapping him between at least one gunman and the encroaching flames. "May as well give up."

Smoke clawed its way down his throat, and he fought desperately against the need to cough. He didn't dare make any sound that would give away his position as he crept stealthily up the hillside, the crackle of the flames helping to mask any sounds he might make moving through the underbrush.

"It's over, McAvoy. If you want your daughter back, you'll come out now."

He lowered his head for a moment, squeezed his eyes closed to alleviate the burning and reminded himself they would never release Lily, even if he did surrender himself. The only way to save her was to evade them and find her as quickly as possible. He moved his hand slowly, pulled out his weapon and listened for the voice.

"She's here with me. Right now," he taunted. "Come and get her, you coward."

No way would they have a hostage with them. She'd be tucked away somewhere, probably nearby, so they could use her as leverage, then eliminate her as soon as they took him out.

"I'm going to shoot her right now unless you come out of hiding!"

He pinpointed the voice. To his right. Not far. He gathered his feet beneath him, keeping his head low, then started toward the sound in a crouch. He could only pray Avery wouldn't fall for the ruse and expose herself. And he couldn't help feeling like a hypocrite. He'd turned away from God, probably when he'd needed Him the most, only to turn back in a time of need. *I'm sorry. I wouldn't ask for help for myself, but for Avery and our daughter, I must. Protect them, Lord.*

Storm kept pace at his side, glancing at him occasionally for any further commands.

Flames engulfed a tree to his left, forcing him toward his attacker. That was fine. Better to confront him now, when he knew exactly where to find him, than to flee and risk the possibility of an ambush later on.

A twig snapped ahead of him. Avery? A second gunman?

He froze, pressed his back against a tree and surveilled the forest. Thick trees, an overabundance of summer brush and the layer of smoke hindered his vision. He squinted as he scanned the forest, peering between branches and anything else a predator could use as cover. Then he spotted a patch of white. Avery? No, she'd been wearing jeans and a green T-shirt, which would provide her at least some cover as long as she ignored the taunts from their pursuer and remained hidden. *Please, stay put, Avery. Please, trust me.*

His heart skipped a beat at the knowledge that she wouldn't. How could she trust him? How could he even ask her to?

Tristan shifted for a better view. He wouldn't shoot anyone without warning, but he had to be sure he was in a strong position. The instant he called out, he'd lose his tactical advantage. He crept forward, keeping the white patch in his sight. When he had a clear view of a tall, bulky man in a white T-shirt, he aimed his pistol. Since the guy was carrying an automatic weapon, it was safe to assume he wasn't a hunter or a civilian trying to escape the growing fire.

"Freeze! Or I'll—"

The guy swung the weapon toward him even as he opened fire, with no concern for anyone or anything else that might be in the forest.

Tristan pulled the trigger, and the guy went down. He moved quickly in case a second attacker was lying in wait. Tears pooled in his eyes from the thick, black smoke, blurring his vision. He squeezed his eyes shut, then wiped the tears away, steadying his aim. When no further shots were fired, he ran hunched over to the man and checked for a pulse. Tristan's bullet had only torn through the guy's shoulder, but he'd hit his head on a boulder when he'd fallen and lay unconscious.

Tristan patted him down for weapons, a sense of urgency begging him to move faster. He removed a handgun from a holster on the guy's belt, then confiscated the machine gun and slung it over his head and onto his back. He reached for his cuffs as he slapped the guy's face a few times to bring him around.

Storm spun and barked, the thick hair on the back of his neck standing up like a mane.

Tristan whirled, weapon drawn, just as a second gunman emerged from the woods.

The guy held a submachine gun pointed straight at him. He lifted the weapon and grinned.

Before he could open fire, Avery stepped from the woods behind the guy and nailed him in the back of the head with a thick branch, then ducked out of the way.

The guy staggered and turned toward her.

Tristan fired, his bullet finding its target in the man's side, and he dropped.

Flames engulfed the nearby trees, erupting in a massive wall of fire. With a loud crack, an enormous tree went down, partly in the clearing, partly caught against other trees. Flames jumped and danced, eager to consume whatever fuel they encountered.

"Avery!" They were out of time. "Run!"

He lunged for her, grabbed her hand and called Storm to heel. His muscles screamed in protest as he shoved Avery ahead of him and scrambled up the hillside, using roots and branches to pull himself up the steeper inclines. He stopped to boost Storm onto a plateau, then hooked Avery's arm and half pulled, half shoved her ahead. He didn't dare look over his shoulder at the wildfire threatening to devour everything in its path—including the three of them.

THREE

After escaping the gunmen and hiking the mountain for hours, Aery stumbled and went down onto her hands and knees amid scattered pine needles and dead leaves, then simply stayed where she was, sucking in deep, greedy breaths of the sooty air and the moldy scent of mulch. Despite the fact that they'd outrun the fire—for now—and their pursuers hadn't attacked again, she still didn't feel safe. Night had fallen, the darkness made worse by the layer of smoke blocking any light the moon or stars might otherwise provide, also hindering their navigation abilities. And they were forced to trek the wilderness based on memory and some idea of where the fire was behind them. Unless, of course, the wind blew the embers and a new fire popped up, which had already happened several times.

Tristan fell beside her with Storm at his side.

Smoke burned its way down her throat, brought tears to her eyes, made it difficult to breathe. Gasping, she sat back on her feet, shoved back the long, soot-covered strands of hair that had escaped her ponytail and stuck to the blood drying on her temple, and closed her eyes. She worked to slow her racing heart, to control the gut-wrenching fear that chased her no matter how far or how fast she ran. Her eyes shot open. "We have to keep going."

"We will. But we need a minute to regain our strength, or we won't make it the rest of the way to Jansen's ranch." Tristan rolled from his knees to his back, then lay spread eagle in the small clearing, staring up at the sky. Streaks of black covered his face, tear tracks running through it all. He swiped at the tears, smudging the mess across his cheeks.

Storm dropped down next to him, pressing his massive body against Tristan's side, and dropped his head onto Tristan's arm.

He reached over and wove his fingers into the dog's thick, black mane. "We'll take five minutes, regain our strength, and then I'll call again and find out how far out we are and when we can expect the extraction team."

She couldn't argue with him, no matter how badly she wanted to. If she didn't stop for a minute, she was going to collapse, and she'd be no good to Lily at all. "You think they'll still come, right?"

"Yes. They're already close by, just waiting for me to give the signal that we've almost reached the extraction point and won't have to detour."

They'd heard sirens earlier, and for a while they'd been able to see the flashing lights of emergency vehicles in the distance behind them, but she hadn't heard a thing in the past hour or more. Even the normal nocturnal sounds seemed disturbingly absent from the night.

Tristan squeezed his eyes tightly closed. When he opened them, he sat up and folded his legs.

Storm shifted to rest his head on Tristan's lap, then nudged his hand until Tristan began to stroke his side with such affection it nearly broke Avery's heart. And she was happy he'd at least found someone to love. But was Storm his only companion? It didn't matter now.

"Can you tell me something about what she's like?" he asked quietly.

"Lily?" Just saying her name brought a wave of grief.

He nodded, his attention firmly riveted on Storm.

"She's amazing." Her voice hitched, and she had to take a moment to regain her composure.

Tristan waited, his gaze still averted.

"She's smart, and funny, and kind. And she's outgoing. And creative. And fearless. I'll never forget the day I found her standing at the top of the stairs with a beaded necklace hooked over the railing." The memory still brought a twinge of unease, even though things had ended up fine. "She jumped up, determined to zip line down the railing. Thankfully, I was close enough to catch her before she tumbled down."

A sad smile played at the corner of his mouth. "That courage will serve her well."

She could only pray he was right. A sob escaped, and she had no hope of containing the welling emotions any longer. "She's my whole world."

Tristan knelt beside her, wrapped an arm around her shoulders, offering her the strength she'd need if she was going to get back up and keep going. "It's okay, Avery. We're going to get her back."

"You don't think they…" She couldn't bring herself to ask the question plaguing her every thought.

"No." He set her back, scooted around to face her and gripped her upper arms. "Look at me. Please. Look into my eyes so you'll know I'm telling you the truth—about this, at least."

She did as he asked, lifting her gaze to meet his, willing

herself not to fall for his promises. And yet, she wanted so badly to cling to the hope he offered.

"They won't kill her." He looked so sincere, as if he truly believed that with all his heart.

She squeezed her eyes closed. "You can't know that."

He shook her gently, bringing her focus back to him. "Listen to me. As long as I'm alive, no harm will come to Lily."

"How can you be so sure?"

"Because they are using her as a tool. If they do anything to her, hurt her in any way, they lose any leverage they might be able to hold over me. They know she's their only chance of flushing me out. While we do have other evidence against them, I'm the only undercover agent who can testify firsthand to who their leader is and what I've seen her do. Including commit murder."

"You saw her kill someone?" Shock warred with fear.

"Yes." He clenched his jaw so tightly she thought his teeth might shatter, then swallowed hard.

"Why didn't you just arrest her then?" She couldn't begin to imagine how much he suffered having witnessed someone commit murder. The fact that he hadn't shared the killer's name wasn't lost on her. And she didn't push. She was probably better off not knowing.

"Because I was undercover, surrounded by thugs who were completely devoted to her. She allows very few people into her inner circle, and all of them are a hundred and ten percent loyal. They'd kill for her, take a bullet for her, do a stint in prison for her—whatever she expects or orders."

"Except for you." She couldn't help the fear that the image of him surrounded by the kind of people he'd described elicited. But she shoved it aside—had to if she was going to function knowing the monsters he'd described were the same people who now held her daughter hostage.

"Yes. I can't be bought. I can't be frightened away. And I had no family to lose. At least, that's what I thought. That's why I went in. It took two long, hard years undercover for me to move up the ladder and make it to the top of the organization. As long as I'm alive, their entire operation is in jeopardy. If they can't eliminate me, they will no doubt throw my character into question somehow, with some planted evidence that makes me look dirty."

His expression turned rock hard, no lingering trace of the guy she'd known. "Without me…chaos. Our confidential informants will all turn tail and run, and who could blame them? The physical evidence we've amassed will all be questioned, so we'd basically end up with nothing. Judges, lawyers, jurors can all be bought, scared off or disappeared. Our case hinges on me testifying. And once we put away her operatives that are about to face trial, we'll go after her. Hopefully, facing life in prison, someone will give up her whereabouts."

She nodded, sniffed, wiped away the tears. The stranger standing before her was confident, brave, fearless, it seemed. No matter what he might have been through these past five years, no matter what kind of atrocities he might have witnessed, nothing could change that fact. It was all she had, so she'd just have to hold on to that. In the meantime, she couldn't stay still another moment. Especially now, having more of an insight into the people who'd taken her daughter. As long as she was moving, she was moving toward Lily. She stood and brushed off the debris clinging to her jeans. "We have to go."

"Avery…" Tristan stood and reached for her hand.

She froze, contemplating his offer of comfort, desperately wanting to accept, but at what risk if she allowed her heart to open, even the slightest bit, to him? She turned away and started walking. She'd been alone for a long time, with no one to depend on but God, and it was time she got back to that. She began to pray as she walked. Prayer led to reflection. And she couldn't help but wonder, had God's answer to her original plea for help been to send Tristan? How ironic would that be, if it turned out the man who'd broken her heart would be the one to save it now?

Storm walked beside her, glanced up, then nudged her hand with his head.

"What do you need, boy? Comfort? A friend?" She laid her hand atop his head as she'd seen Tristan do—easily, since the K-9 stood as high as her waist—and started up the trail. At least the going was less difficult now that they were on a walking trail rather than hiking through the brush. "I know how you feel, buddy."

Tristan walked a bit behind her and Storm, and Avery wasn't sure how to feel about that. On one hand, she needed the space. On the other, it would be so easy to lean on him. He seemed so strong now. So sure of himself, confident in a way he hadn't been when she'd known him.

When she'd last seen him, as he'd kissed her goodbye and driven away with a promise to return, his parents had just been murdered. He hadn't believed the sheriff's claim that their deaths had been senseless, a random mugging in a town where the only violent crime was an occasional bar fight.

Ten days later, he'd shown up at her house early one morning, when her grandfather was in the middle of a coughing fit and needed a breathing treatment and she was battling what she suspected now was her first bout of morning sickness, and announced he was leaving. Ten days since he'd grown colder, more distant, more consumed by grief. No matter how she'd tried to reach him—despite mourning the couple who'd treated her like their own daughter, had not only accepted her but loved her—he'd refused to accept any comfort from her, refused to offer any comfort in return. She'd understood, even then, that he'd had nothing to give. Yet, watching him lose himself in the bottomless well of grief and helplessness had broken her heart. Would knowing about Lily have helped him heal?

She hugged Lily's blanket against her and inhaled, desperate for some connection to her little girl. But all she could smell was the smoky residue that clung to everything.

"Can you pinpoint my location?" Tristan spoke quietly into the SAT phone as they walked. "No. I'm not sure if we'll still use the same extraction point."

Avery had no choice but to trust that Tristan knew what he was doing. She didn't have to like it, but she did have to concede he understood more about what was going on than she did. And even if she didn't trust Tristan with her heart, she did trust God. If He'd sent Tristan, there had to be a reason for that. Even if she didn't yet know how it would bring Lily back to her, she had to hold on to the hope that it would. She stopped and waited for him to catch up.

"It'll depend on what we find." He paused, held up a finger for her to wait, then frowned and resumed his conversation. "Yeah. Yeah. Got it."

She waited for him to disconnect the call, then asked, "What's going on? Did they find Lily? Why aren't they coming for us?"

"No, they haven't found Lily yet. I'm sorry." He stuffed his phone back into his pocket and studied something in the direction of the fire's orange glow.

Sheer terror gripped her throat, cutting off her air supply. She gasped in a small breath, and pain tore through her. Was Lily down there?

"Hey?" Tristan wrapped an arm around her. "You okay?"

She nodded and, for just one moment, allowed herself to take the comfort he offered. She sank against him, her entire body trembling, and he pulled her into his embrace, cocooning her in safety, sheltering her from harm. She closed her eyes and breathed in deeply. Beneath the odor of smoke all around them, another scent came to her, woodsy, familiar, the scent of nature and long afternoons spent hiking in the woods. Was it real? Or the lingering memory of a time long past, a time when she'd thought her life was perfect? Unfortunately, she now knew that time had been nothing but an illusion.

She straightened away from him.

He released her instantly, the eyes she'd once gazed into with complete adoration now filled with pain and heartache.

But there was nothing she could do about that. "I'm sorry. I just..."

"Hey, you have nothing to be sorry for. A lot of people would have already crumbled under the kind of pressure you're enduring right now." He swiped a hand over his mouth and looked around. By the time his gaze returned to her, any emotion she might have found there had been carefully masked. "I'd like to try something. I'm not sure it'll work, especially since we have no idea if they took her in a vehicle, but I'd like to try to have Storm search for Lily."

Hope flared. "Yes."

"It will be dangerous. That fire could change direction and cut us off at any moment. Plus, I was forced to let our attackers go when we fled the flames. They could be anywhere." He traced a finger along her cheek, then tucked a few stray strands of hair behind her ear.

She resisted the urge to tilt her cheek into his hand and ignored the spark of sentiment the gesture brought. The last thing she needed right now was emotional baggage weighing her down, interfering with whatever decisions she might have to make. "Do you think they escaped?"

He shrugged. "No way to tell unless they come after us again or the firefighters find them."

"Will someone let you know if they do?"

"Yes. If they're found, my team will be right there to interrogate them."

She nodded, praying that would be the case and that one of them would tell them where Lily was being held, but in the meantime… "I don't care how dangerous it is. If there's a chance of finding my little girl before this whole forest goes up, then I'll take it. What do we have to do?"

He studied her another moment, seemed to accept she was okay to do whatever needed doing, then nodded and turned all business. Any sign of the tenderness he'd shown only a moment before gone. "Is that blanket Lily's?"

She lifted it. "Yes."

"Storm can use it to try to find her. But we may have to backtrack toward your house for him to pick up the scent, and the fire seems like it might be moving in that direction."

"I don't care." She ran her fingers along the silky edge

Lily liked to rub against her cheek while she drifted off to sleep. "I'll do whatever it takes to find Lily. But the blanket smells like smoke now." A fact that brought a pang of heartache.

"It won't matter. A Newfie's sense of smell is estimated to be between a hundred thousand and a million times more sensitive than ours. If Lily's out here, and we can pick up her trail, Storm will be able to find her, but…" He hesitated.

"But what?"

He heaved a sigh. "If we wait, and the house goes up in the fire, we'll have missed our chance."

"Whatever it takes," she choked out in a raspy whisper, the words burning their way up the back of her throat. She squeezed her eyes closed for a moment, prayed they'd find her in time, then reluctantly held the blanket out to him. Nothing could have been more difficult than entrusting that last piece of her daughter to him.

"Okay." He took the blanket from her, so gently, almost reverently, and averted his gaze. "My team will be ready to extract us when I call, no matter where the search takes us."

She nodded. That was the least of her concerns. Unless they found Lily, she wasn't leaving anyway. But it was probably good that one of them was able to think ahead.

"Storm." He held the blanket out for the Newfie. "Find."

The big dog scented the blanket, then began sniffing around the clearing. He lifted his nose in the air and sniffed.

"Search."

Tristan looked toward the fire. "We'll start moving in

the direction of the house and see if he's able to pick up the scent."

"Okay, what do I have to do?"

He gestured slightly behind him. "Stay right on my heels. Whatever happens, do not stray. Try to stay as quiet as possible, so we don't give away our position if anyone is trying to find us. If you hear or see anything, just get my attention. With the visibility up here, it will be easy to lose you, and if I have to redirect Storm to search for you, it'll take precious time away from the search for Lily."

She nodded her understanding and moved just behind and to the right of him, then laid a hand on his shoulder. She'd cling to him like glue if it meant a chance at finding Lily. "Is this okay?"

"It's perfect."

For the first time, they were actually moving in Lily's direction instead of fleeing their pursuers. Hope filled her.

"Please, God, help us find her," she whispered, then added silently, *And thank You for sending Tristan.*

Together, they turned toward home and the inferno blazing not far enough in the distance.

They'd been walking for close to an hour since Tristan had given Storm Lily's blanket to scent. He still held the soft, delicate cloth in his hand, not because Storm needed to scent it again, but because Tristan needed it to hold on to, as if his entire sense of hope clung to that one small scrap of fabric.

I'll find you, Lily. I won't leave this mountain until I do.

He shook off the fear that dogged him as they hiked. It wouldn't do him any good. If anything, it might hinder his ability to do what was necessary to find his child. *His child.* No matter that Avery kept referring to Lily as hers.

That didn't make a difference to him. She wasn't wrong, after all. He'd abandoned her, left her alone.

He considered Avery's childhood and felt even worse for leaving her. Her grandfather had done everything he could to make her happy growing up, but he couldn't make up for the parents she'd lost. Then, he couldn't help thinking about his own parents, so loving, so devoted, so close to him and to each other. Lily deserved that same love, that same devotion, that same whole family. Would he have returned to Timberwood Falls if he'd known about her?

He wished he had an answer to that. Who knew? Maybe he was afraid to search too deeply into himself, afraid he might come up short of the man he wanted to be, the man his father and mother had raised. What would they think of the way he'd run away, left Avery, whom they'd adored, alone and frightened and grieving?

But he simply hadn't been able to stay after they were gone. He couldn't bear the thought of their killer roaming free, despite Sheriff Reynolds's assurances that they were actively investigating and certain they'd find their killer. He'd pedaled the same excuses time and time again, for five years, every time Tristan called to check in. But had Reynolds even looked? His insistence that their murderer must have been a transient, someone just passing through town, fell on deaf ears. Tristan wanted answers, and he wanted justice.

It was that sense of purpose that had led him to the FBI, that had pushed him to become a member of an elite team that investigated missing persons cases. He'd considered other teams, but this was the right place for him, the perfect place. Because, at least with his unit, there was sometimes a happy ending and they could bring someone home to their loved ones. Unlike the conclusion to his own family story.

Avery stumbled beside him, gripping his shoulder tight to keep from going down.

He reached out a hand to catch her, then called for Storm to take a break. Not that the dog needed one yet, but Avery was starting to slow, despite her best efforts and determination not to give up. He wished they had water, but there were no nearby streams in the direction they were headed, a straight line toward Avery's house. They'd have to stock up on supplies once they got there.

He led Avery to a half-rotted stump and gestured for her to sit. "We'll take a break for a couple of minutes."

"No, I'm—"

"Storm and I need to rest a minute, too. We're no good to Lily if we miss something out of exhaustion." He leaned against a nearby tree, cradled his aching ribs.

She nodded and sat, silent, thoughtful, beautiful.

Not that he hadn't always found Avery attractive—with her long blond hair alight with highlights, jade eyes speckled with browns and golds, and brilliant smile—he had. But it was her inner beauty that called most to him, her kindness, her ability to love so completely, so selflessly. The way she loved Lily now, the fact that she'd no doubt die on that mountainside before giving up on her daughter.

She'd loved him that way once, too. And had he appreciated it? No, he'd turned his back on her and run away. Like a coward. Because of what he couldn't face. And the trust he'd once seen in those eyes had turned to suspicion. "Avery. I'm so, so sorry."

She glanced at him then lowered her gaze. "What are you sorry for?"

"Leaving the way I did. I—"

"Tristan." She held up a hand to stop him, then stood and brushed herself off. "It doesn't matter right now. Nothing does, except finding Lily."

"Please, Avery. Just give me one minute to say this, and then we'll move." Timberwood Falls would never be home for him again. He'd left for a reason, and that reason still existed. As much as he'd like to have a relationship with his daughter—if they found her—his and Avery's time together had come to an end long ago. He'd never again allow her, or anyone else, to get close.

He couldn't. Not after everyone he'd ever loved had been lost to him. His parents, whom he'd adored, had been taken from him. Their murders had indirectly cost him Avery, whom he'd loved dearly—probably still did if he were being honest, in some deep part of him he'd closed off in order to survive. And now, thanks to him, the daughter he'd never even gotten to know had been taken as well. No, him loving anyone, allowing anyone too close, was just too costly, not only for him but for everyone else involved. Avery deserved better than that. She deserved someone who could open up and love her the way she loved. And that someone wasn't him. He'd do well to keep the wall he'd constructed around his heart shored up tight.

He started to reach for her hand, then thought better of the idea, the gesture too intimate. As much as he hoped he and Avery could maybe find their way to friendship, and that she'd agree to him spending time getting to know Lily, he didn't want to give her the wrong impression. Instead, he stuffed his hands into his jeans pockets. "I just wanted you to know how sorry I am for leaving the way I did."

She shrugged. "It doesn't matter."

"Yes." Forget any impression it might give. He reached for her, squeezed her hand, then returned his hand to his pocket. "I couldn't stay here anymore. With my parents' murders unsolved, I couldn't even stand walking through town, wondering if every person I came face-to-face with had killed them. I'm not sorry I left. I had to leave. And I knew you couldn't with your grandfather's cancer diagnosis. You had to stay to take care of him."

"It still would have been nice to have been offered the choice," she said softly.

"I know. You're right." And he'd been selfish, too afraid she'd ask him to stay and he'd give in and do so. So, he'd simply told her he was going, promised to come back, then kissed her goodbye and left. It wasn't lost on him that she didn't try to say she'd have gone with him. They both knew better.

He'd only learned of her grandfather's death on the chopper flight to Timberwood Falls. Mr. Taylor had been a kind man, filled with love for his granddaughter. "I'm sorry you lost him."

"Thank you," she said softly. Her chin trembled as she made a visible effort to fight back tears.

"But I should have talked to you, explained why I couldn't come back. I should have returned your calls. I shouldn't have left you hanging with the promise to return like I did. I just—" Just what? Wanted to hold on to the innocence and love they'd shared? Hadn't wanted to sully it with honesty and regret and the promise of a future without her, a future alone? Or, if he was honest with himself, had the problem been that he'd known he'd come back to Timberwood Falls if he spoke to her, known he wouldn't be able to resist? And bitterness, resentment and anger would have festered for the rest of his life until they finally consumed him. At least now he could spend his life helping others. He might not have been able to save his parents, might not have even been able to bring their killer to justice, but he could save as many others as possible as a tribute to their memory.

He sucked in a deep, shuddering breath that brought a stab of pain, though whether physical or emotional, he had no idea. Then he let it out slowly. This conversation had gone so much better the million times he'd rehearsed it in his head over the years. "Anyway, I just wanted you to know I'm sorry I hurt you."

"It's okay, Tristan." She sniffed, wiped the tears spilling down her cheeks. "I'm sorry, too. I should have told you about Lily. And I wanted to. I just… I wanted to tell you in person, not send you an email or text saying, 'Hey, by the way, you're going to be a father.' Plus, I figured if you knew about your daughter, you'd probably feel forced to come back. And I guess I selfishly wanted to know you were returning because you loved me and Lily, not because you felt obligated. So, I'm sorry, too."

The range of emotions battering him weighed heavily, but there was no time to examine any of them now. "So, does this mean I'm forgiven?"

"I forgave you a long time ago."

He nodded, opened his arms and gave her an awkward hug, the past five years like a gaping chasm between them, then released her and stepped back. "You good to go?"

"I am, yes."

"All right. Let's move." Because they were running out of time to find Lily. And it was easier to fall back on his training than to deal with feelings he had no idea what to do with.

They started off, Avery's hand loosely gripping his

shoulder, as if she was afraid to lean too heavily on him. Not that he could blame her. While he'd managed the fumbling apology, he'd done nothing to heal the rift between them. Who knew? Maybe that was beyond repair.

At least he'd come to understand why she hadn't told him about Lily. As much as he wished she'd handled things differently, and appreciated her apology, he couldn't really blame her for wanting to tell him face to face. And it wasn't her fault he hadn't returned her calls.

It didn't take long to reach the field behind Avery's home. He held out a hand to stop her and Storm, then scanned the perimeter of the clearing. Thankfully, the fire hadn't reached the house—yet. But if the wind shifted even a little, the flames would engulf everything in their path, including the house. They needed to get supplies and get out of there. But first he had to make sure no one was waiting to ambush them. He gestured for Storm to stay, then leaned close and whispered in Avery's ear, "I'm just going to check the perimeter, make sure no one's here."

She nodded and crouched low in the brush beside Storm, her arm resting across his back.

It didn't take long to run a quick circle of the perimeter, keeping just inside the tree line to avoid detection. He needn't have worried. The area was deserted, though he could hear shouts and radio calls from the firefighters in the distance. Their attackers probably figured they wouldn't be stupid enough to return with the fire raging so close, embers already falling onto the lawn, some igniting into small flare-ups. They obviously didn't know him as well as they thought they did.

He returned and crouched beside Avery. "We need some supplies. A backpack, if you have one. Water, a bowl for Storm. Everything I had with me went up with the car."

She nodded and stood.

"It would be better if I went alone and you stayed here with Storm."

She contemplated him for a moment, her eyes filled with uncertainty.

How was he supposed to keep her safe if she wouldn't trust him? "All right, come on. But we get in and out as quickly as possible."

She nodded.

"Storm, come." It was best to bring Storm in with him, anyway. They knew Lily had been in the house, so he would pick up her scent there and see where it led. If whoever took her had kept her nearby, which Tristan suspected they would, he'd find her. Knowing they didn't plan to keep Lily alive, why bother making arrangements for a place to hide out and risk being caught with the child? Better to just take cover somewhere close and dispose of her once they had what they wanted. Unless, of course, they planned to sell her to the highest bidder. But would they risk that? When she might be able to identify them? Might remember something and tell someone? It wasn't like Lily was an infant. And it pained him that he had no idea what his little girl might be capable of.

Storm stopped suddenly halfway across the clearing. He turned, sniffed, then barked once to signal he'd picked up Lily's scent.

FOUR

The second they entered the house, Avery reached for the light switch.

Tristan laid a gentle hand over hers and simply shook his head.

Right. She should have thought of that. Anyone could be concealed under the cover of darkness. What would she do if they couldn't end this quickly? Even once they got Lily back, they wouldn't be safe until everyone involved was in prison. How long would that take? Would she ever get used to life on the run, to the crosshairs on her back at all times? She shook off her unease—had to if she were going to keep moving. She stepped carefully through the front door into the house, her footsteps crunching loudly over the glass scattered across the floor from the windows that had been shot out.

When she reached the kitchen, she grabbed the pink canvas backpack she used for hiking from the pantry, contemplated its contents, then refrained from dumping it out in order to make room for her most prized possessions. The first-aid kit, flashlight, portable charger and bear spray would no doubt come in handier than some of the more sentimental items she might want to save. As much as she wished they had time to hose down the house and lawn, they didn't. Really, the whole area should have gone up already, but thankfully the wind had sent the flames skirting her property as they raced up the mountain. She could only pray her distant neighbors had fared as well and that the firefighters could contain things before there was too much damage.

Pain squeezed her chest as she moved through the house. Even in the dark, everything was a constant reminder of Lily. She inhaled deeply, searching for the comforting scent of home, and was met only with the cloying odor of smoke that permeated everything. Instead of wasting time worrying about what she'd have to leave behind, she nudged aside a pang of grief and tossed Tristan a second backpack, the blue one that had been her grandfather's. "Help yourself to whatever you need. I'll be right back."

"Only take what you absolutely have to," he called after her.

She waved over her shoulder to acknowledge the advice but kept going up the stairway. Her eyes had adjusted to the dark, and she knew the layout of the home she'd lived in her whole life. She ran to her bedroom closet first, keyed open the fireproof box and removed a handful of documents—birth certificates, Social Security cards, the deed to the house—and stuffed them into the bag. No sense wasting space taking the box.

Without hesitation, she quickly removed two photos from the frames on her nightstand, one of Lily as an infant on the day she'd brought her home from the hospital, the other a selfie the two of them had taken amid a fit of giggles one cold, sleepless night as they'd snuggled together beneath the patchwork quilt. Her hands shook, and she lost her grip on one of the frames. It clattered against the wood floor and shattered.

Instead of wasting precious seconds picking it up, she simply left it where it was and stuffed the photos into the bag with the documents. She thought about the few things her grandfather had given her that had belonged to her parents, a bracelet her mother had left behind when she'd run off, a letter she'd written him from some far-off land and a picture of her with Avery's father, all smiles and waves. But Avery bypassed the drawer and headed for Lily's room. There simply wasn't time to waste on sentimentality.

She grabbed the teddy bear Lily always slept with from the bed and a small raccoon plushie she often rubbed against her cheek when she was upset, crammed them into the bag and zipped it up. It wasn't much, but the familiar toys might bring her daughter some comfort once this ordeal was done. Without sparing a glance at the rest of the room she was forced to leave behind, she swung the pack onto her back and slid her hand along the smooth, hand-carved banister her grandfather had made as she jogged down the stairs. When she reached the living room, Tristan already had her grandfather's rifle in hand. She unlocked the cabinet and took out several boxes of ammunition, then added them to a compartment on the side of the pack she could easily reach in a hurry.

Tristan spared her a quick glance, all business. "You ready?"

If any sense of nostalgia had gripped him upon entering the home, it didn't show in his neutral expression. Had the surroundings stirred any memories? He'd certainly spent enough time there with her when they were young. Did he notice the subtle changes she'd made to accommodate Lily and to make the house more her own? Considering the darkness and the current situation, probably not.

But she remembered his childhood home, always so warm and cozy, filled with the aroma of freshly baked desserts. She clung to memories of the evenings spent sipping hot cocoa in front of the fireplace with Tristan and his mom and dad. All of those things had been lost to him when his parents had died. While she wished he'd decided to stay, she could certainly understand why he'd had to leave. How difficult would it have been for him to stay in the home he'd shared with his parents? What would it have felt like for all of that warmth and love to have disappeared, for his home to be cold and empty? A stab of grief hit hard, her emotions complicated by feelings of both betrayal and compassion.

She shook glass shards off the purse she'd left by the door, fished her wallet out and whipped out her driver's license, credit and debit cards, and, for some reason she couldn't explain, her library card and added them to her pack. "Yup. I'm ready."

Was she really, though? Ready to go find Lily, yes. Absolutely. But ready to leave behind her home? Maybe have to start over again? No. Definitely not. But it didn't matter now. They would find Lily, and they would make it off this mountain. She could rebuild everything else as long as she had her daughter.

"Let's go." Seeming to sense her hesitation, Tristan gently hooked her elbow and guided her away from the past. Instead of leaving through the front door, he cracked open the French door, its glass still mostly intact, that led to the back deck. He shifted into the shadows and held up a hand for her to wait.

She did, practically vibrating with nervous energy,

though she had no idea what he might be able to see from where he sheltered. All she could see were the silhouettes of trees, the orange glow illuminating the night behind them, and the smoke billowing overhead.

He took a moment to offer Lily's blanket to Storm again, then followed the big dog out.

Avery closed the door behind her without looking back. If she did, she might lose her precarious grip on her emotions. She followed Tristan off the deck and across the yard, then breathed a sigh of relief as they entered the forest and the shadows enveloped them, hopefully shielding them from view.

She stayed on Tristan's heels, fearful of losing him amid the smoke, but she didn't reach out, didn't grip his shoulder as she had earlier.

He glanced back every so often to make sure she was behind him. Since she didn't know the protocol and didn't want to interfere with Storm's search, she remained quiet. She couldn't help but wonder if Tristan's thoughts, like hers, had wandered toward the past, toward a time when the two of them had hiked these same forest trails. She could still envision sunlight dappling the path rather than embers dancing in the sky. If she dared close her eyes for a second, she could almost smell the fresh scents of pine and wildflowers rather than the sickly smoke invading her lungs. She'd been so innocent then, so naive, before she'd been so hurt. Instead of the roar and crackle of flames, she remembered the soft whisper of the wind through the trees, the bird and insect songs, the dull rumble of the waterfall in the dista—

The realization of where they were headed slammed into her like a physical blow. "Wait."

"Hold." Tristan issued the order then stopped and turned to her.

She sucked in a shaky breath, choked on the smoke. Tears tracked down her cheeks, and her eyes stung. "Do you remember the cave behind the waterfall?"

He nodded, his expression somber.

"It's not that far from here, in the same direction Storm's headed."

Tristan nodded and pressed a finger against his lips.

She lowered her voice to barely a whisper, stepped closer to him. "Do you think that's where they're holding Lily?"

He squinted in the direction she'd indicated, obviously remembering exactly where the falls were. "It would make sense. A good place to hide with little to no chance of being seen with a child that doesn't belong to them."

She sensed he was holding something back but didn't push it. The sooner they got moving, the sooner she'd get to Lily. She didn't ask if he thought she was still alive. She already knew what he'd say. And she had to believe it was true, had to believe they wouldn't harm her child if they wanted Tristan to cooperate. "You will do what they're asking, right? If we find her, you'll agree not to testify."

A pained expression crossed his face before he lowered his gaze from hers.

And she knew. He wasn't going to give in to their demands. Not even to save her daughter—to save *his* daughter. Pain tore through her, a stabbing agony so deep she had no hope of easing it. Even if she knew in her head these killers would probably not agree to such a simple exchange, she needed to know Tristan would at least try if there was even a remote chance it might save Lily.

"I'll get her back, Avery. Now, stay quiet and let's

move." Then he started forward without another word, and she was left to either follow him or be left behind. Again.

Until that moment, she'd been so certain she'd never again know betrayal like she'd felt when he'd left. But she'd been wrong. Because that was nothing compared to the sense of betrayal that cut through her now. She dug in and grabbed his arm to stop him then hissed, "Promise me you'll do or say whatever it takes to get Lily back. I need that, Tristan."

Tristan grabbed her upper arms and drew her close, cutting off any further thoughts, which was probably for the best. He pressed his cheek against hers in an awkward embrace and whispered against her ear, "Listen to me. No matter what you think of me, I promise you I *will* get Lily back. If sacrificing myself would save her, I would do it in a heartbeat. But it won't. And you may as well understand what we're up against here. This isn't some game to get me to keep my mouth shut. Their goal is to eliminate any witnesses, immediately, with no more concern than swatting at an annoying fly."

She gasped as the full impact of his words and the stark honesty in them slammed through her.

He eased her back a bit, just enough to capture her gaze with his. "You need to understand that. And if you get the chance, you grab Lily and run. You keep going without ever looking back. Do you understand?"

Did she? Could she run and leave him? Yes. For Lily she could. She would. She'd have to. But what would it cost her? And how would she live with herself afterward? *God, please don't let it come to that.*

He released her and held out a hand. "Give me your phone."

Struck numb by the weight of his words, she simply took it out of her pocket and handed it over.

He added a number to her contacts and passed the phone back to her.

"Valerie Robinson? Who's that?" She ignored the twinge of something that too closely resembled jealousy.

"She's my assistant director's right hand. If you and Lily are forced to escape without me, you call that number and tell Val what happened. She'll see that you get whatever help you need to get Lily out of here and keep you both safe." He turned away from her then and shrugged off his backpack, dug inside and came out with a water bottle. He took a long swallow then held the bottle out to her.

Since she couldn't seem to get words past the lump clogging her throat, she forced down a few sips. It didn't help.

Tristan filled a small bowl with the remainder of the water and set it down for Storm.

He lapped it up greedily.

"Tristan, I'm sorry, I…" But what could she say? That she didn't want to hear the truth about the men they were up against? That she couldn't bear the thought of having to leave him behind? That she was sorry for not trusting him to put Lily first? What reason had he given her to? He'd come. It was that simple. He'd come when she needed him most. And that's all that should matter. She had no doubt he was good at his job, and he'd already proven he was a good man who would risk everything for her and Lily. If there was a way to get them all out of this, he would find it.

"You have nothing to be sorry for." He lifted the bowl the instant Storm finished and returned it to the pack, then used a rag from her kitchen to wipe his eyes before tucking it into the back pocket of his jeans and hefting the pack back on. "I wish there was time to spare your feelings, Avery, but there isn't. You have to understand what we're up against and the possibility you might have to get out of here with Lily on your own. Agreeing not to testify isn't an option for me, on so many complicated levels, but I will not let my…" He heaved in a deep breath, his emotions peeking through for the first time since he'd returned, and his voice shook. "I will not let Lily die. No matter what it takes to save her, you have my word I will do it. Now, let's go. We're wasting precious time we don't have."

She watched as he strode down the familiar trail into the forest, then followed after him. She'd wanted honesty, and that was exactly what he'd given her. At least now she understood the stakes.

But Storm never wavered, simply kept moving forward in a direct path toward the waterfall.

As they drew closer, the dull rumble of water tumbling over rocks that she'd always found so peaceful roared menacingly.

Storm left the trail to weave between the trees.

Tristan followed with full focus and determination, never sparing a glance toward her as they moved forward, his head on a constant swivel as he crept through the brush. But she had no doubt he knew she was right behind him, even though she didn't make a sound. It seemed he was aware of every inch of his surroundings.

She'd do well to pay the same full attention. She forced everything aside, blanked her mind, used the sounds of the falls and the river churning beneath to center herself, to help her concentrate. Then she listened past it for any other sounds that might warn of an ambush.

The smoky sky had begun to turn from black to a sooty gray, probably as close to sunrise as they were likely to get with the fire still raging. They needed to move faster, needed the last remnants of darkness to conceal them from any lookouts. If they were even in the right spot. The thought that she and Lily often walked to the falls occurred suddenly, but she didn't dare make a sound to tell Tristan. Could Storm have picked up Lily's scent from her hikes with Avery? Disappointment surged. How could she have made such a foolish mistake? Because she was thinking too emotionally. She needed to calm down, to focus, to think clearly.

Tristan held out a hand for her to stop then motioned for her to duck behind a thick pine.

Storm followed Tristan's hand signals and did the same.

Tristan crouched behind a chokecherry thicket and pulled a pair of binoculars they used to bring along to spot wildlife from the backpack. He must have either found them or remembered the cabinet her grandfather had always kept them in.

Sadness threatened to overwhelm her. Since she had no hope of shaking it off, she simply embraced it instead.

He adjusted the lenses then studied the terrain, slowly scanning their surroundings, then lowered them and gestured her to move to him.

She did as instructed, her heart hammering. Had he found Lily?

"If I could leave you here, I would," he whispered.

She started to bristle.

"But I need you to grab Lily if we find her. You remember what I said?"

She nodded. It didn't mean she'd do it. If there was a way to save both Lily and Tristan, she would. But there was no point in arguing with him right now.

"Stay close to me."

She nodded again and stuck to him as he and Storm crept through the brush parallel to the well-worn path leading up toward the top of the falls. Large boulders lined the river's shore, and she could clearly recall images from her past, jumping from rock to rock with Tristan close behind, laughing when they missed a step, enjoying a dip in the cool water along the edge, sitting with Lily and tossing pebbles far enough out to watch them disappear into the rapidly moving currents.

When they reached a level clearing, thankfully not very far up, he stopped, took his backpack off and left it concealed in the brush. He waited for her to do the same, then took out his gun and waved for her to move directly behind him and let Storm lead the way.

She held her breath, then pressed her back against the rocks, braced herself against the cool spray and inched along the narrow ledge that would lead to the cave opening. It wasn't the first time she'd done so. She used to enjoy the peace and solitude sitting behind the falls brought. She slid on the slick surface, and her gaze shot to Tristan even as she quickly regained her footing. Hopefully, the roar of the falls would mask any sound they might make.

When he reached the opening, he tapped Storm's back and the big dog stopped in his tracks. Tristan leaned past him to peer into the cave.

Avery held her breath. *God, please, let her be here and safe.*

He yanked his head quickly back and laid it against the

hard rock wall, squeezed his eyes closed for a moment and blew out a slow breath.

When he looked back at her, she mouthed, *Lily?*

And he nodded.

Relief rushed through her, buckling her knees and nearly tumbling her over the ledge into the rapids below.

Tristan lifted an arm across her to keep her from going over.

Grateful, she leaned her back against the rocky wall, pressed her palms against the cool, damp surface behind her and uttered a prayer of thanks as the tears she had no hope of controlling escaped and poured silently down her cheeks.

Tristan, his back braced against the wall, envisioned the scene he'd only had a second to glimpse. A child—Lily, he knew from her picture, *his* child—lay still, eyes closed, on the ground. He had no time to acknowledge the emotions coursing through him, threatening to overwhelm him with the potential to cause him to make a costly mistake. So he buried his feelings deep and focused only on the matter at hand—rescuing his daughter.

A man sat with his back against a large boulder, no more than two feet from her, automatic weapon held loosely across his lap. Thankfully, his eyes had been closed, and he hadn't seen Tristan.

Tristan was confident he could neutralize that threat without harm to the little girl. The second man posed more of a problem as he paced back and forth in front of the falls, his attention riveted to his phone screen. He was awake, alert and in the way.

Tristan couldn't move, since any advance warning

would alert Lily's captors to his presence and end any hope of getting to her without a gunfight.

Okay, first things first. He had to get past Storm and couldn't do so on the narrow ledge in view of the cave entrance. He motioned Avery back a few feet.

She reluctantly moved.

A pang of regret tried to surface. He had no time to coddle her, though he spared her a quick glance that he hoped conveyed a confidence he didn't fully embrace. The cave sat fairly low on the waterfall, but it cut deep into the hillside. There could easily be more men hiding out of his line of sight. He could only hope these were the same two men who'd taken Lily and that they didn't have reinforcements. Taking out two of them to reach the girl would be difficult enough. He considered retreating, calling for backup. Getting Avery to withdraw was doubtful. But it was the best option.

He managed to move past Storm and gave him the hand signal to stay, then leaned back as far as possible and flared his senses. He couldn't risk another peek into the cave. He'd have to keep track of the men's movements by sound, let instinct guide him. He shot off a quick text to Val with their location and the fact that they'd found Lily, then tucked his phone away. She'd have backup on the way in a heartbeat. The only question was, could he wait?

He looked past Avery. Thousands of embers whirled and danced in the sky. They were running out of time. The encroaching fire was going to force his hand.

"Well?" one of the men asked, pulling Tristan's full attention back to the cave.

Tristan held his weapon at his side and strained to listen.

"She texted that two of our men are down and Mc-

Avoy is still somewhere on the mountain," his associate responded.

"Alive?"

"Gee, I don't know, numbskull, but I assume so, otherwise why mention it?"

Hoping the men were too occupied with each other to notice him, Tristan risked a quick glance into the cave. The man who'd been sitting had stood, leaving his weapon on the ground beside Lily. With both hands on his hips, he faced off with his companion, who still clutched his automatic weapon.

"Can we get out of here now?" he whined. "I don't want to get caught up in that fire, and this place gives me the creeps. How do we know there's not a grizzly back there somewhere?"

"Rossi said to stay put until she calls back, and I ain't crossing her. Even you can't be that stupid."

Since the other man remained silent, Tristan had to figure his companion was right.

Gianna Rossi was calling the shots, just as he'd known, but it was good to have it confirmed. Now there was one more thing he could use to put the woman away. A top adoption lawyer in the Pacific Northwest with incredibly vast resources at her disposal, Gianna's greed had led her down a dark and dangerous path. Instead of being content to legally unite children with the parents who desperately sought them, Gianna had turned to a life of crime. Now the woman commanded a veritable army of minions who kidnapped children and sold them to the highest bidders, no matter whom they might be or what sinister intentions they might have. No way could he accept even the remote possibility Lily might end up that way.

"Yeah, well, that's easy for her to say," the guy tried

again. "She's sitting in her cushy office while we're stuck here in this damp, snake-infested cave."

"Knock it off, Mitch. You saw one snake."

"It was a *rattlesnake*." The man's voice bordered on shrill.

Things were escalating out of control. Tristan was going to need to intervene before Mitch decided to go rogue and get rid of Lily himself. Of course, Mitch wouldn't last long after that. If there was one thing Gianna Rossi didn't tolerate, it was disobedience.

He'd wait as long as he could for Val to work her magic. He didn't dare look back at Avery, certain she'd pressure him to move. But at the moment, it was safest to wait. Lily appeared to be sleeping. He replayed the scene again, assured himself the twitch he'd seen was real. She was alive and as safe as could be for the moment. There was no sense risking her life just yet, despite the impatience emitting from Avery in waves.

"Get a grip, man. It's not—" A cell phone rang, cutting the guy off. "Hang on while I get this. Yeah?" He paused. "Okay, got it."

"Was that Rossi?" Mitch asked.

"Yeah."

"And?"

"Looks like you're going to get your wish. She says to teach McAvoy a lesson and get rid of the kid, then try to get the woman for leverage."

No time to wait.

"It's about time she—"

"Freeze!" Tristan stepped from behind the wall, signaling for Avery and Storm to wait. He leveled his weapon in front of him, aimed in the direction he'd seen the guy with the phone and the gun.

"McAvoy." The guy lifted his weapon and fired. Shots ricocheted off the cave wall an inch from his head as he ducked.

Tristan prayed Avery had stayed put even as he pulled the trigger. Then again. Two shots sent the guy tumbling over the ledge, through the falls and into the river below.

Then he whirled on Mitch, who'd used Tristan's momentary distraction to grab his own weapon and yank Lily up by the arm. She sagged limply as he wrapped an arm around her and clutched her against him, blocking any shot Tristan might have.

Tristan had one moment of terror like he'd never known when Lily didn't wake. Then the rapid rise and fall of her chest registered. And he noticed how tightly her eyes were squeezed shut. Playing possum? Smart kid.

"One move and I'll kill her." Mitch managed to get his weapon aimed at Tristan. "Lower your gun. Now!"

Storm surged to Tristan's side, planted his front feet apart and growled deep in his throat.

Tears streamed down his little girl's cheeks.

Tristan weighed his options—no easy task with Lily in the way and Avery sobbing softly behind him. Since the guy was using Lily as a shield, Tristan had no shot. But the instant he lowered his weapon, Mitch would take him out, then Lily and then Avery and Storm. No way could he let that happen. He had to at least buy enough time for Avery to get away with Lily and Storm. And the only thing keeping him alive right now was the gun he held steadily aimed at Mitch's forehead. If the guy so much as twitched, Tristan would fire and take him down. Should he take the shot anyway? He'd probably hit his mark… He inhaled, long, slow, increased his pressure on the trigger, then eased off as Mitch hefted Lily higher. What if she twitched? Lifted her head? Jerked? He just couldn't take the chance.

Mitch used his weapon to gesture toward the back of the cave. "Put the gun down and get back there. The woman, too."

Lily's eyes shot open, and she sobbed the instant she spotted her mother.

"And keep that dog with you, or I'll shoot it and then the kid." Still, his weapon remained aimed at Tristan.

Though he didn't release his hold on his handgun, Tristan inched toward the back of the cave, searching for any opening. Once he'd moved far enough in, he kept his gaze riveted on Mitch as he gestured for Avery to pass behind him and deeper into the cavern.

He could feel the tremors as Avery followed his instructions, moving closely behind him.

"The gun!" Mitch yelled. "Now!"

"Listen to me, Mitch. I can help you," he reasoned. "If you agree to testify, I can—"

A bark of laughter assured Tristan that was not happening. "Sorry, dude, I like living too much to cross Gianna Rossi."

"Okay, then just drop the gun, Mitch, and let the girl go. It's not like your companion is here to rat you out. Rossi will never know. This is your last chance." Tristan took another step closer. He'd only have one shot, and he had to be close enough—couldn't misjudge by so much as a fraction of an inch.

A slow grin spread across Mitch's face as he edged toward the exit. If he sidestepped another inch, he'd be out of range.

"Okay," Tristan agreed. "Fine."

Mitch stopped moving.

"I'll lower my weapon, just please put Lily down." Tristan took a casual step forward, started to crouch as if he were about to relent and abandon his weapon. "You'll earn favor from Rossi for killing me. There's no need to harm the girl. Just let her mother take her out of here. They'll disappear, and Gianna will never know you let them live. You have my word."

"Aww, come on, now, McAvoy. You gotta know that ain't how this ends."

And because he did know, Tristan pounced without warning. He dropped his weapon to free up both hands, came up beneath Mitch's arm and grabbed hold of his wrist. A quick twist and snap broke the wrist and sent his weapon clattering to the ground.

Mitch screamed but didn't go down. Nor did he release Lily, even as she struggled against him. Keeping a firm grip on the child, he landed a hard kick against the side of Tristan's knee.

Tristan staggered back, lost his hold on Mitch's wrist.

When Mitch lunged for his weapon, Tristan reached it first and kicked it over the edge into the falls. Ignoring the sharp stab of pain, he followed through with a knee to Mitch's face.

Mitch stumbled away, went down on one knee.

Storm barked wildly but stayed clear of the fight.

Where was Avery? He had to reach his weapon. He caught sight of her in his peripheral vision, scrambling toward his gun.

"Don't even bother, Avery. You won't have time to get to the gun and shoot me." Mitch's grin and the humor dancing in his eyes sent a chill racing up Tristan's spine. He froze and watched in horror as Mitch tossed Lily over the ledge into the river below then bolted toward the exit.

Storm lunged toward the man, barking wildly, but stopped abruptly when Avery screamed.

Then she plunged over the ledge after Lily.

When he turned back, Mitch was gone. Tristan started after him, but stopped abruptly. He had to get to Lily and Avery. As much as it killed him to let Lily's captor escape, his little girl needed help. Training triumphed in a hard-won battle over instinct as he fought the urge to dive in after them. All of them in the water would solve nothing, only add to the problem. "Storm, save!"

FIVE

Avery came up from under the water sputtering, just in time to see a large black blur launch through the falls from the cave ledge. Storm! Then she lost sight of him, searching frantically for her daughter as the rapid current carried her downstream. Her hip smashed into a boulder, bringing a flash of pain she acknowledged then ignored as she ricocheted off. Water splashed into her eyes, and she swiped at them, trying to clear her vision enough to see.

She'd gone in immediately after Lily, and she was heavier. Surely she would overtake her. Right? She had to be close. Keeping her bearings, she tried to avoid the obstacles she could see and rebounded off the ones she couldn't, letting the water carry her as it would Lily. "Lily!"

Lily's answering scream brought a wave of relief. She was alive. But only for the moment. Lily could swim. Avery had made sure of that, had begun teaching her as an infant. But the rough water would be too much for her. She might have the knowledge, might even be completely comfortable in the water, but she wouldn't have the strength to battle the current and the rough surf for long.

Avery inhaled to yell again, sucked in a mouthful of water and choked.

"Mama!"

"Lily!" *To the right.* She spotted her barreling downstream, struggling to keep her head above the surface. Avery angled herself toward the shore, aiming to come up ahead of Lily, and started to swim. Strong, sure strokes propelled her quickly toward her daughter. She squeezed her eyes closed against a face full of water rebounding off a boulder, then opened them as quickly as she could and shook the water from her eyes as she continued to swim toward her daughter.

Then Lily went under.

Noo! With her gaze glued to the spot she'd last seen Lily, Avery swam harder. She sucked in as much air as she could and then dived, holding her breath until her lungs ached and begged for air as she searched beneath the surface. She rolled and tumbled with the current. Her shoulder slammed into a sharp rock, and she barely resisted the urge to gulp for air. Then she spotted Lily a few feet away. She reached for her, kicked harder, had to breathe, desperately needed air…

Her hand closed over Lily's shirt—*oh, God, thank You!*—and she pulled her close even as she kicked upward. The instant her head broke the surface she gasped for air, sucked in more water and choked it up. It didn't matter. She had Lily. She clutched her daughter against her, letting the current drag her as she struggled to keep Lily's face above water.

Lily beat at her, screamed, waved her arms in a frantic attempt to free herself.

"Lily! It's me." Avery sucked in more water, spat it out. Water hit the rocks, sprayed off, stung her face. She ignored it. She couldn't get her child turned around, so she hugged her tightly, Lily's back against her chest, and pressed her mouth close to her daughter's ear. "Stop fighting, Lily. It's Mama. I have you, baby. I have you."

"Mama?" Lily went limp in her arms, then started to sob. "Mama."

Avery simply held on, cradled her little girl and tried to shield her from the rocks and branches, some submerged, hidden obstacles beneath the surface, as best she could. She was going to have to swim for shore. But she needed a moment first, just one second to calm herself, assess the situation and be grateful for her daughter's weight in her arms.

"Oh, God, thank You," she whispered and closed her eyes against the sting of water and foam as she offered a prayer of thanks. She opened her eyes, searching for an escape from the fast-moving current.

And then Storm was there, nudging her with his nose.

Tristan ran along the shore toward them, screaming and waving his arms. He cupped his hands around his mouth and yelled to her. "Avery! Have Lily grab on to Storm!"

She didn't want to let go, didn't dare release her hold, but she was going to have to swim. Was there a way to do so with Lily in her arms? No. She was already exhausted, and Lily had to be as well.

"Give Lily to Storm!" Tristan ran hard, hurdled branches, vaulted over boulders and kept pace as they rocketed downstream.

They had to get out of the water. She couldn't do it alone. "Lily. Can you hear me?"

Lily nodded.

Okay, that was good. Not only was she awake and alert but able to respond.

Storm swam alongside them, circled around, returned.

"I need you to grab on to the dog's neck. Can you do that?"

Lily didn't respond.

Storm circled again.

Avery's strength waned. *Not yet, please. Just keep me strong a little longer. Please.* "Lily, wrap your arms around Storm's neck. I'll be right here. I promise."

Avery held her breath, waited. The instant Lily reached for the big dog, Avery used the last of her strength to heft her onto his back.

Storm immediately swam for the shore.

Lily wrapped her arms around his neck and clung tight.

Avery tried to keep pace, struggled to keep up with the dog. Her arms and legs ached from battling the current. Bruises, cuts and abrasions begged for attention. Her head pounded along with the roar of the falls. Still, her gaze stayed on Lily as Storm reached the shore and scrambled out of the water with her little girl still clinging to his back.

Relief sent a wave of nausea rushing through her. The adrenaline subsided, leaving her shaking, sapping the last of her strength. She started to go under.

"Storm, guard!" Tristan yelled.

Was his the last voice she'd hear? A sense of peace settled over her as she started to drift. If nothing else, she'd managed to save Lily. And Tristan would see her safe, even if—

Something grabbed hold of her arm.

Her eyes shot open, and she found herself staring up into Tristan's brilliant blue eyes, filled with fear he quickly masked.

He gritted his teeth and held tight with one hand, gripping the branch of a felled tree with the other as he braced himself and struggled to maintain his hold and guide her toward shore.

She summoned the last of her will, reached up and grabbed a branch, then let him help her use the branches to pull herself out of the deepest water and move toward the shoreline. When she finally reached the shallow-enough edges, she tried to stand. Her legs turned to rubber, then buckled. "Lily."

Tristan wrapped a strong arm around her, kept her from going down and comforted her, much as she had Lily. "I've got you, Avery. Lily's fine. Storm has her, and he won't let her walk away or go back into the water. Just take a second—sit, catch your breath."

"I can't. I have to get to Lily." But she had no choice. Her legs wouldn't carry her any farther. When they gave out, she fell to her knees and crawled the rest of the way out of the water. Then she turned around and leaned against a boulder, sucking in deep, greedy gulps of smoky air that burned her lungs. When Tristan lifted her in his arms and carried her to where Lily and Storm waited, she didn't argue.

He set her down gently in the grass.

Lily flung herself into Avery's arms and cried.

Storm whimpered and sat beside them, his side pressed against her and Lily.

She heard Tristan talking to the big dog, his tone comforting and reassuring, but his words didn't register, her concentration too fully focused on Lily.

"Oh, baby." Avery smoothed a hand over her daughter's hair, held her close, rocked back and forth. "It's okay now. I'm here, and I have you, and no one is going to come near you again."

She had to set her back, had to examine her, had to

make sure she wasn't injured, but she couldn't bring herself to let go. Not yet. So she simply held on, eyes closed, comforted by the familiar feel of Lily in her arms, the scent of baby shampoo lingering just beneath the stronger odor of smoke…

Smoke! The fire! Her eyes shot open. Millions of embers floated with the wind, scattered like stars against the inky backdrop.

A hand dropped onto her shoulder, and she jumped and whirled, clutching Lily tighter.

Tristan lifted both hands as if in surrender. "Sorry. I didn't mean to startle you."

"No. I'm sorry. It's okay. I guess I'm just jumpy." If that wasn't the understatement of the year… "Thank you, Tristan."

"Of course. It was the least I could do." Pain filled his eyes as he stared at his daughter, seemingly at a loss for what to say or do. His gaze deepened from the usual dazzling blue to a dark and stormy gray. Or perhaps that was just a lingering effect of the smoke. He held Lily's blanket out to her.

The girl sank against Avery, glaring at him with suspicion, and popped her thumb into her mouth—a habit she'd broken more than a year ago.

"It's okay, Lily. This is…" *This is who? Tristan? Daddy?* What was she supposed to tell her daughter about the man who'd just saved them, the man who'd been the love of Avery's life at one time, the man who'd left them behind and never looked back? Lily had never asked about her father, perhaps because she'd been too young. Would she have eventually? Probably. And considering she'd be starting school soon, more likely sooner than later. And Avery would have been honest with her, as she'd always vowed to be. But now? Under these circumstances?

Avery reached for the blanket, brushed her fingers against Tristan's, and something like a shock coursed through her. Something she'd do well to ignore in her current state lest she mistake gratitude for anything more. Setting aside any lingering feelings she might or might not still have for Tristan, she took the blanket from him and handed it to Lily.

The little girl hugged it against her and, with one more harsh glare for Tristan, buried her face between the blanket and Avery's chest.

"I'm sorry, Tristan, she's just—"

"Please. Don't." He held up a hand to stop her, pain and regret deepening the lines bracketing his clenched jaw. "It's fine. She doesn't know me, and after what she's been through, she has no reason to trust me."

"As soon as we get her settled..." She'd what? Tell her little girl the truth? Then how would she explain it to her when Tristan disappeared again? Which he certainly would, considering he'd made a life for himself after he'd left Timberwood Falls. But what if he didn't leave? What if he decided to stay a part of his daughter's life in some capacity? Could she dare hope for that? "We should go."

He nodded and silently extended a hand.

She took it, let him help her up and looked around. "Do you know where Mitch went?"

He shook his head, swallowed hard and scanned the immediate area.

"I'm sorry I didn't get to your gun. I tried—"

"It's okay. I had to leave it behind. I didn't dare waste a second going after you and Lily, but I'm going to go back for it in case Mitch is lying in wait somewhere, but

I doubt it. If he's got half a brain, which I sincerely doubt, he's halfway to anywhere Gianna Rossi won't be able to find him right now."

"You think she'll go after him?"

"Of course she will. He failed her. And between us, there is nowhere Rossi won't be able to find him. Her net is vast, worldwide, her minions many and her resources limitless." He rubbed a hand over his five o'clock shadow and moved closer to Avery's side. As they started to hike back upriver, he called Storm to heel.

When the big dog slid between them, Avery moved over a bit to allow him room then laid a hand on his head and whispered past the lump clogging her throat. "Thank you, Storm."

He looked up at her through soulful, dark brown eyes as if he understood, then bumped her hip with his side and kept walking.

Avery hefted Lily closer and kept her head on a swivel, though she suspected Storm would alert them if anyone was lying in wait. Still, shadows dotted the forest, deep and dark enough to conceal a predator, human or otherwise. "Do you think he'll try again, then? Mitch, I mean."

Tristan sighed, long and deep, then simply looked at her over Lily's head, nodded and kept moving.

Once Tristan retrieved his weapon, he tucked it back into its holster and hurried back out of the cave. He didn't want to leave Avery and Lily alone any longer than necessary, but the little girl had started screaming when they'd started back toward the cave, so he'd been forced to leave her and Avery tucked up between some boulders, concealed as well as possible, though the child's cries would certainly have alerted anyone in the vicinity to their whereabouts. He'd left Storm with them, though he'd be little use against someone wielding a weapon.

And, truthfully, Tristan had needed a moment, just a fraction of a second to wrap his head around the fact that this beautiful child was his daughter. And that she was terrified of him. A stab of pain cut deep. Not only because she couldn't yet trust him, but because of what she'd been through at such a tender age—being ripped from her home, held at gunpoint by strangers. Well, he couldn't change the past, but he'd do everything in his power not only to keep her safe from here on out, but also to make her feel secure and protected.

He stood on the ledge for a moment and scanned the area for possible snipers. Just because he'd kicked Mitch's weapon over the falls didn't mean the guy didn't have another stashed somewhere nearby, especially since he'd fled rather than try to reach Tristan's weapon. Nor did it mean he didn't have reinforcements. Although, with the fire bearing down on them, it would be safer to retreat and try again later. Safer for Avery and Lily as well. As much as he'd like to take Storm and try to track Lily's kidnapper, his priority had to be their safety. Which meant it was time to go.

He jogged back down the trail toward where he'd left Avery hiding. Since he'd already called in their location and the fact that they'd recovered Lily, backup would be there momentarily. And he couldn't help feeling grateful his team would arrive soon. Not because he couldn't handle Mitch, but because he needed the familiarity of people he trusted surrounding him. And, if he was being honest with himself, which he always tried to be, he needed the buffer between him and Avery.

He was too close to this case. He couldn't think clearly

enough. The emotional roller coaster he'd been riding since he'd received Avery's first frantic message had taken its toll, had messed with his head, had hindered his ability to rely on his instincts. An ability that had kept him alive for the two years he'd spent undercover with Gianna Rossi's organization. Two years when he'd been another person, the kind of person who ignored many of her illegal pursuits, though he'd stopped short of allowing anyone to be kidnapped on his watch. Whenever he'd gotten wind of a potential kidnapping, he'd alerted his team and they'd intervened.

Unfortunately, that intervention eventually alerted Rossi to the certainty that she had a mole in her midst. And when she'd ultimately uncovered the person she'd thought responsible—her only henchman other than Tristan who'd known about the operation—she'd called a meeting. Before Tristan even knew what was happening, never mind had time to react, she'd shot Jeff Cabot in cold blood, then ordered Tristan and another thug to clean up the mess.

Would Tristan have intervened if he could have? Absolutely. He'd have given himself up in a heartbeat to have saved that man's life. Even if he was guilty of a multitude of crimes, he hadn't been guilty of the one that had gotten him killed. That had been Tristan. And Cabot's blood was on his hands. Something he had to live with every day.

As if he didn't already shoulder enough guilt. Because Cabot wasn't the only person he hadn't been able to save. Three agents had disappeared, most likely tortured and killed by Rossi's goons, in an operation Tristan had been responsible for. While all of the deaths weighed on him, it was Benny that hurt the worst, cut the deepest. Benny,

Storm's original handler, was a dear friend. And now he was gone. Because of Tristan.

"God, forgive me," he whispered softly.

"What?" Avery looked up at him. Did he dare hope that was a glimmer of trust he noted in her eyes?

And if it was, did he deserve it? Probably not.

"Nothing. Sorry. I was distracted." Great. An out-of-control fire raging toward them, a gunman on the loose and hunting them, and the head of a major crime ring determined to see them dead. And he was distracted, haunted by the past. No *probably* about it—he definitely didn't deserve her trust. "We have to go."

She nodded and tried to stand, no easy task with Lily clinging to her neck for dear life, her legs wrapped tightly around her mother's waist.

Not that he could blame her after all she'd been through—thanks to him. Some father he turned out to be. When he reached out, Avery simply shook her head and leaned on a boulder to keep her balance. "I've got it, thank you."

It was probably for the best. Why should she lean on him when she'd surely gotten used to being on her own in the years since he'd abandoned her? Why would she let herself depend on him, probably assuming he'd walk away once this was over? For a moment, just a snapshot in time, he allowed himself to wonder what would happen if he stayed. An image played in his mind, him and Avery hiking in the mountains, the air clear and fresh, fields of wildflowers spread before them, Lily between them holding hands as they swung her high amid a fit of giggles.

A sniper on a ridge, his crosshairs on Lily, on Avery. The reality of his life slapped him in the face, and he shook off whatever foolishness had gripped him in that instant. "My team is meeting us a couple of miles up the mountain, but we've got to go now."

She nodded and clutched Lily tighter.

The fairy tale he envisioned in that moment might not ever come to pass, but somehow he'd remain a part of his daughter's life. He wouldn't abandon her a second time. A smile tugged at him. He might have missed her first four years, which would always hurt, but he had the rest of his life to make up for that. First, he had to get her somewhere safe. "Storm, heel."

The big dog obeyed instantly, trotting between him and Avery, his senses alert.

Avery glanced at Tristan, then frowned and nodded toward the encroaching flames, probably not wanting to scare Lily any more than she already was.

"It'll be okay." The reassurance was meant for both of them, though Lily simply kept her face buried against Avery's neck. "We're headed the opposite direction of the flames."

"Okay. Good." She fell quiet then, striding alongside him, their footsteps echoing against the brush and leaves like shotgun blasts in the unnatural silence that had enveloped the mountains.

He wanted to apologize. Again. Wanted to say something to ease the uncomfortable awkwardness that had fallen between them. But he had no idea what to say. So, instead, they simply hiked quietly up the side of the mountain with him reaching out a hand now and then to help her over any more difficult obstacles and her uttering a subdued, "Thank you."

He kept watch on Avery in his peripheral vision as they walked—the way she soothed Lily without even seeming to give it any effort at all. Could he ever be that comfortable with his child? Would Avery even tell Lily he was her father? Did he want her to? Yes. He might not know much else about his future, but he did know that. He'd failed Lily and Avery once, but he'd see them protected in the future.

"How long have you had Storm?"

"Huh?" The question, after such a long period of quiet, caught him off guard and pulled him from thoughts better left unthought.

"Storm." Avery gestured with her elbow, since she cradled Lily in both arms. "How long have you had him?"

"Almost a year. He originally belonged to another handler, Benny Regan." Who'd disappeared, along with two other agents, when they'd raided Gianna Rossi's headquarters after she'd murdered Jeff Cabot. Since his body had never been found, they could only assume Benny had been taken by the few of Gianna's thugs who'd gotten away during the raid. Most likely, he'd been tortured then killed. That wasn't unusual for those who crossed Gianna Rossi. Had he given up Tristan's identity? They had no way to know, so Tristan had been pulled out and tucked away while they'd built their case and he took over Benny's position as handler and trained with Storm.

"He's really amazing." She shifted Lily into one arm long enough to reach down and scratch Storm's head. "How did you end up with him?"

He started to wave it off, hadn't spoken about Benny since the failed raid, then decided an honest answer was the least he could give her. "Almost a year ago, I witnessed Gianna Rossi..."

He trailed off when Lily turned her head to study him, thumb in her mouth, blanket tucked between her and Avery.

"Um…"

Avery simply nodded her understanding that he couldn't share the gruesome details.

"There was nothing I could do to stop what happened, but once I was able to remove myself and report to my team, we went back to arrest her." He chose his words carefully, fully aware of the weight of Lily's stare. "When we arrived, Rossi was already gone, but she left a veritable army behind. Seven agents were badly injured in the raid. Storm's handler, Benny, a very close friend, along with three others, weren't as fortunate. We were only able to recover one of the four."

"And Benny and the other two?"

He shrugged and shook his head. What could he say? They could only assume the worst, considering the condition of the one agent's body they'd been able to recover several weeks later, and nobody held out any hope of recovering the three missing agents alive. "And it was my fault. Somehow, I got the intel wrong. I was so sure she'd be at the offices, so confident we'd get her. And I was wrong. And Benny and ten other agents paid a heavy price for my mistake."

And the guilt had practically eaten him alive for the past year.

She reached for him then, just a gentle brush of her fingers against his arm. "I'm so sorry, Tristan."

The fact that he could tell she truly meant it choked him up. Then again, Avery had always been blessed with an overabundance of compassion. He nodded his appreciation. "Anyway, I took Storm. Since Benny and I had trained together, Storm knew me. Plus, I was just coming off a long-term undercover assignment, so logically it was a good choice."

He didn't bother offering what he suspected, that his boss, Assistant Director Noah Charles, had assigned Storm to him because he'd felt like Tristan needed him, needed someone to take care of. He'd never know that for sure. But Noah had an uncanny knack for knowing what each of his agents needed, and Storm had saved him. Having someone to care for, someone who depended on him, had kept him from spiraling into a dark place he might never have recovered from. Had having Lily done that for Avery when he'd left her? "I'm sorry, Avery. I really am, for the past, for all this."

"You've already said." She offered a weary smile. "And I'm really glad Storm is yours. He's a hero."

"Yes, he is." The sound of a motor nearby saved him from having to say anything else, which was probably for the best, considering he had no idea what else to say.

He pulled his handgun and gestured toward a dense patch of sagebrush.

Thankfully, Avery understood and quietly followed his instructions, stepping behind the thick foliage.

Lily, perhaps realizing something was wrong, popped her head up and stared at him, eyes wide and filled with fear.

Pain gripped his heart, squeezed, and he wanted nothing more than to reach out to her, to reassure her everything would be okay. Instead, all he could do was put a finger in front of his lips and pray she wouldn't cry out and give their position away before he could check out who was coming.

Avery whispered something in her ear, and Lily nodded, then she disappeared from view as Avery ducked out of sight.

Shaking off an abundance of what-ifs, Tristan held a hand out to the side, palm down, paused, then lowered it.

Storm dropped down to his belly.

Tristan crouched low, weapon aimed straight ahead as he scanned the area. It sounded like at least two vehicles were approaching, and it should be his team. Val had already texted they were nearing the retrieval site, and he'd almost reached the clearing that would serve as their extraction point, but he couldn't be too careful with Lily's and Avery's lives on the line.

He crept forward, using the thick brush as cover, breathing in the acrid smoke and fighting the urge to cough.

Storm belly crawled beside him, head down, ears perked up and alert.

When the two vehicles, a Humvee and a Suburban, bounced over the rugged terrain and rocketed into the clearing, Tristan breathed a sigh of relief. Now all he had to do was get Avery and Lily safely into the Humvee and off the mountain and then he could set out in search of Mitch, Gianna Rossi and the rest of her organization and finally put an end to this nightmare.

The fact that Rossi had still managed to keep her business up and running, thriving even, despite having to go into hiding, stung. And it was time to end her reign of terror.

He stood and waved as the vehicles rocked to a stop.

Two of his fellow agents, Oliver Knight and Isabella Anderson, jumped from either side of the Humvee, automatic weapons held ready.

Storm jumped to his feet, whirled and barked once, just as a child's scream tore through the forest.

Lily!

SIX

Avery sensed a presence behind her even as Lily screamed. She flung an arm up just in time to keep a thick branch from hitting her head full force, but the blow still partially connected with her temple, rocking her. One knee twisted, and she went down on it, still holding Lily tight.

When a fist crashed into her jaw, her hold loosened as she reached out to balance herself against a tree trunk to keep from toppling over.

She needed to fight back but couldn't without risking losing her hold on Lily. She hugged her daughter tight against her, shielding her from Mitch's attack as best she could, and prayed help would come in time.

Mitch pressed a booted foot against her hip and shoved as he ripped Lily from her arms and bolted in the opposite direction.

Avery fell back, smacking her head against a rock, then ignored the pain as she rolled over. She lurched to her feet, staggered for a moment, then took off running after the blur that had once again taken her daughter. But this time, he wouldn't get away, because this time he'd left her conscious. She dug in, vision hazy, nausea threatening, and ran. When she tripped over a stray root, she belly flopped, landed spread eagle amid the carpet of dead leaves, then pushed up and dragged herself to her hands and knees. As she regained her footing, Storm raced past her.

She glanced over her shoulder, just as Tristan scooped a hand beneath her arm and yanked her to her feet. "Stay there."

"But—"

"Stay with her," he tossed over his shoulder as he released her and kept running.

Avery braced her back against a massive pine tree, squeezed her eyes closed for a moment to regain her balance, then took a deep breath and blew it out slowly. She'd be no good to Lily if she passed out. Plus, it would take resources away from Lily's rescue if someone had to stop to help her. She had to stay on her feet, had to reach her daughter. Okay, she could do this. She opened her eyes, and everything stayed put. No dizziness. The nausea was still there, but there was nothing she could do about that right now, and it wouldn't hinder her ability to go after Lily.

A man surged past her, then a woman, both carrying weapons and moving way faster than Avery could hope to in her current condition.

Still, if Tristan thought she was going to sit down, wait there and play the victim, he could just think again. She would let the agents do what they were trained for, but she was going to get to her daughter. She started after them.

A man fell into step beside her, probably an easy jog for him. "Cayden Vaughn, ma'am. FBI Missing Persons Unit. You sure you don't want to sit this one out?"

A dull ache radiated through her chest, robbing her of breath. Her head throbbed relentlessly with each footstep. "No way."

"There's no need to rush." He smiled, his brown eyes warm and reassuring. "Storm will get to him before any of us even get close."

Huffing and puffing too hard to answer, she nodded and kept going.

When a man started screaming, she ran faster. Until Cayden grabbed her arm, then she skidded to a stop and bent at the waist, sucking in deep, greedy gulps of air.

Mitch was on the ground ahead of them, rolling in the brush and leaves, screaming for someone to get the big dog off him.

Storm clutched Mitch's ankle between his teeth in an iron grip, growling and moving with the man as he tried to scramble away. No matter which way he turned, Storm clung tight.

"Give her to me! Now!" Tristan was bent over Mitch, who had a firm grip on Lily.

With a sob, Mitch glanced between Tristan and the other two agents standing over him wielding automatic weapons, seeming to weigh his options, then finally relented and released his hold on her.

Tristan stood, Lily clutched against him, and backed away. "It's all right, Lily. You're safe now. Da— Uh… I've got you. I'm a police officer. And I'm going to bring you to your mama."

Lily's entire body stiffened in Tristan's arms as she wailed.

"I gave you the kid, now get this dog off me!" Mitch screamed again.

Tristan, who'd already started toward Avery, glanced over his shoulder and casually said, "Storm, release."

Avery ran to him and threw her arms around Lily. "Oh, baby. Thank you, Tristan. Thank you."

He shifted Lily into her arms and backed up, his gaze still locked on Lily. "You don't have to thank me."

"I—" She what? She had no idea what else to say to him, and at the moment, she didn't have the energy for anything other than Lily. The little girl wrapped herself around Avery, squeezing her neck in a grip that threatened to cut off the circulation to her head, still sobbing.

"It's okay, honey. The police have the man who took you, and they're going to bring him to jail. You're safe now." *Thank You, God, thank You.* Because she couldn't imagine a life without Lily, couldn't bear the thought of what might have happened to her had Tristan not been there. Sheer terror made her light-headed. She hugged Lily tighter.

Lily continued to cry, the thumb in her mouth muffling some of the sobs, but she lifted her head to watch the scene unfolding before them.

The other male agent, along with the female agent, had already rolled Mitch onto his stomach, and they were in the process of cuffing him when Tristan leaned over to read him his rights.

Avery's first instinct was to shield Lily's view as they arrested Mitch and hauled him to his feet. But who knew? Maybe her daughter would feel safer if she watched the police take her kidnapper away, saw for herself that he wouldn't be able to come after her again.

"Here. Why don't you sit down with her while we get him out of here." Cayden led her to a tree that had fallen long ago, looked around and gestured for her to sit.

"Thank you, Cayden."

"You bet." Then he took up a position in front of her with his weapon held ready.

And the realization that Mitch wasn't the only threat

hit her like a sucker punch. She drew in a painful breath. Who knew how many other monsters lurked in the shadows, searching for an opening to try to take Lily from her again? They had to get out of there. And go where? She had no idea. She didn't even know if her home was still standing. And could she even return there? After everything that had happened?

"You okay, Avery?" Cayden frowned.

"Yes," she whispered, overwhelmed, not only by what had already happened, but with fear for what might still come. She pushed the thoughts aside—had to if she was going to function. She forced a strength she didn't feel into her voice. "I'm good, thank you."

He nodded and returned to his surveillance.

Avery scanned the horizon to be sure the fire didn't pose any immediate danger, then sat with Lily in her lap. She set her back just enough to look her over, smoothed her hair out of her face, felt her arms and legs. "Did he hurt you?"

Lily nodded, thumb in her mouth.

Anger surged through her, clearing some of the haziness. Lily needed her, and that was all that mattered. "Where? Can you show me?"

She nodded again, touched her arm, her shoulder, her leg. Ultimately, she lowered her head into her hand, way too grown up, as if the weight of the world rested on her shoulders.

Tears she had no hope of controlling slipped out and rolled down Avery's cheeks.

"Are you hurt, Mama?" Lily said around her thumb as she reached up toward Avery's head, brushed her fingers lightly against her temple.

Avery jerked at the stab of pain, then used her T-shirt

to wipe the blood from Lily's fingertips. "Mama's okay, honey."

Was that true? She had no idea, hadn't even registered the fact that there seemed to be blood running down the side of her face until that moment.

She assessed Lily's injuries, an assortment of cuts, bruises, abrasions, but nothing that seemed too serious. Since she had no clean cloth, she would have to wait until they got somewhere other than the forest to clean her up. She tried to pull Lily close again, but Lily had ideas of her own.

She turned around on Avery's lap, squished her back tight against Avery and clung when Avery wrapped an arm tightly around her waist. While her thumb stayed firmly plugged into her mouth, her sobs drifted off to soft sniffles. At least she seemed to have some interest in the chaos happening around them. Surely, curiosity had to be a good sign.

Tristan and the male agent she didn't know led Mitch back down the trail toward the vehicles, while the female agent crouched in front of Avery.

A beautiful woman with sharp, angular features, dark brown hair smoothed back into a bun and big brown eyes framed by incredibly long, thick lashes offered a ready smile. "Hi there, Liliana. I'm Bella. I'm Tristan's friend and a police officer."

Lily cringed back closer against Avery.

"I'm also a medic." Her glance shifted to Avery for just an instant, then back to Lily. "That means I'm kind of like a doctor. Would it be okay if I took a look at your boo-boos?"

Lily tilted her head to look up at Avery, who wiped away her own tears and nodded. "It's okay, Lily. Bella will take good care of you, and you can stay right here on my lap."

She didn't bother looking to the newcomer for confirmation. No way was she letting go of her daughter.

Lily said nothing, but studied Bella and didn't pull away when the medic felt along her arms and legs much as Avery had done. Then Bella pressed on her belly. "Does that hurt at all?"

Lily shook her head.

"What hurts most?"

She tapped the back of her shoulder.

Avery helped turn Lily sideways, and Bella shifted her T-shirt collar to reveal a row of bruises along the back of Lily's shoulder, probably where one of the men had gripped her too hard.

"It's okay, Lily." She spared Avery a lingering gaze. "Nothing looks too bad, just a little banged up from bouncing around in the river, so what do you say we get out of here and go somewhere safe?"

Lily rubbed her shoulder but didn't respond.

Bella gently took her hand and lifted it away from the wound. "I'll tell you what, I'll even see if we can hunt up some princess Band-Aids. What do you say?"

Lily hesitated, studying Bella, then nodded but still clung to Avery's arm.

"Come on, Mom." Keeping one hand on Lily's back, Bella took Avery's arm and shifted her eyes toward the orange glow hovering over the mountain. "If you don't feel dizzy or anything, we should get going. We have a doctor waiting to take care of both of you."

"Um…" But where was Tristan? Wasn't he coming back after leading Mitch to the car? While Bella the medic's presence, and that of Cayden, who was apparently their new bodyguard, offered some reassurance, Avery didn't know these people. She knew Tristan. She wanted Tristan. And she assured herself it was only because he was a familiar face in the midst of mass confusion.

"Don't worry." Bella flashed that killer smile again and hooked a thumb in the direction Tristan had gone. "He's riding with Oliver in the Suburban with the prisoner. Cayden and I will ride with you and Lily in the Humvee. Sound like fun, Lily?"

The little girl turned and wrapped her arms around Avery's neck, then nuzzled her face into her blanket.

"I'm sorry," Avery started. "She's—"

"Hey." The kind agent laid a hand on Avery's arm. "You have nothing to worry about. Come on, now. Let's get you guys out of here."

Choked with emotion, she had no idea what to say, how to convey her gratitude to this team for their help, so she simply went with "Thank you."

"Of course." She helped Avery to stand, made sure she had her balance before moving her hand from Lily's back, then held on to Avery's arm while she walked her back down the trail and guided her to the waiting Humvee.

Though Avery sought out Tristan, she couldn't see him through the Suburban's darkly tinted windows. Still, she was sure she could feel the weight of his stare as she climbed into the Humvee with Lily in her arms.

He was a coward. Tristan glanced in the side-view mirror for the millionth time since they'd left the mountain, keeping a careful watch on the Humvee following them. Cayden had offered to ride in the Suburban with Oliver and the prisoner so he could ride with Avery and Lily, but he'd refused.

What could he say to them? How was he even supposed to face them? To face Avery? And Lily? The little girl, *his* little girl, had eyed him with suspicion and fear, had screamed and pulled away from his awkward attempts to comfort her, to assure her he would keep her safe. What was he supposed to do with that?

The tumultuous emotions he'd been forced to deal with over the past twenty-four hours, not only learning he had a child but then almost losing her, had finally caught up to him. He needed a minute to himself, needed time to reflect, to just breathe.

He shifted, uncomfortable in his own skin.

Thankfully, Oliver pulled into their headquarters parking lot, saving him from beating himself up any further, as if the past several hours hadn't been enough. He checked on Storm in the rearview mirror. He'd been lying down for a good part of the long trip from Timberwood Falls, but now sat straight up, alert, his attention on Tristan lest he issue any commands.

When he caught sight of Mitch in the rearview mirror, his fists clenched automatically, barely suppressed rage pouring through him, and he had to look away.

Tristan scanned the rural area of north-central Montana, its rolling fields and plains a far cry from the mountainous terrain where he'd grown up. Though their main field office was located in the more urban southern area, where mountains still marched across the state, their specialized unit functioned from a fully staffed three-story brick office building in the north. One of the draws for Tristan when he'd been offered the job. If he was going to have to work in Montana, he didn't want the constant reminder of what used to be home, of what he'd left behind, of Avery.

When Oliver braked at the side door they used for prisoners and shifted into Park, Tristan sighed.

"I can take the prisoner if you want." Oliver Knight, with his wavy auburn hair and close-cropped beard, kind blue eyes and boy-next-door look, might seem like a pushover at first glance, but he was more than capable of defending himself and escorting the prisoner to a holding cell. "So you can go with your family."

His family? He had no right to call them that. "Thanks, but I've got it."

Without waiting for a response, Tristan climbed out and rounded the Suburban. Then he opened the back door and let Storm out, all without sparing a glance toward the Humvee that had pulled into the circular drive and up to the front door where it would be safer to get Avery and Lily out.

"You're a good boy, Storm." Storm had done well, and Tristan needed to take the time to reward him properly, to care for him, bathe him, let him rest. There simply hadn't been time—nor was there time now, much to his disappointment. For the past year, while they worked on getting everything in order to prosecute Gianna Rossi if they should ever find her, it had been just him and Storm. It was probably time to get back to that. He petted Storm's massive head. "Heel, Storm."

The dog fell into step with him as they headed to where Oliver was unloading Mitch from the back seat.

Storm stopped when Tristan did and stood tall, ears perked forward, posture alert, in full work mode.

Oliver had Mitch by the elbow, the prisoner's hands cuffed behind his back.

Tristan took the other elbow, caging him between them as they walked him into the building. When an agent opened the door and they escorted Mitch inside, Tristan breathed a sigh of relief. He'd half expected an attack on the way to or once they reached the facility. Although Rossi should have no reason to know where they'd take him, which was why they'd decided on their own base of operations, which housed only their own unit and their support staff, rather than the field office.

Assistant Director Noah Charles strode toward them, the fluorescent lights in the windowless corridor highlighting the stark contrast between his darkly tanned skin and honey-colored hair. When he reached Tristan, he extended a hand. "Tristan. I trust the trip back was without incident."

Since he already knew the answer, considering he'd have been the first one notified if anything had gone awry, Tristan simply shook the proffered hand. "Thank you, sir."

The formal greeting was a sign of respect to be sure the prisoner understood this was the man in charge. Noah ran an informal unit, where the agents were a close-knit group and all called each other by first names. He'd told Tristan on his first day with the unit that he preferred the casual culture. If his agents were to count on each other, have each other's backs and put their lives in each other's hands, they could certainly call each other, and him, by their given names.

Noah aimed a look at Oliver and pointed down the hallway. "Get him processed and set him up in Interview A. We'll catch up."

"Yes, sir."

Noah turned his attention to Storm, petting the big dog's head in greeting. "I hear you're the hero, Storm. Good boy."

Tristan waited while Oliver led Mitch down the corridor, waited for him to turn the corner and get out of earshot. "What's up?"

Noah fished a treat out of his pocket and offered it to Storm, then stuffed his hands into his pockets and rocked back on his heels. "Gianna Rossi surfaced."

Everything in him went perfectly still. "What?"

Storm, probably sensing his sudden tension, leaned against his leg, and Tristan absently reached down to pet him. The action soothed him.

Noah held up his hands. "It was only for a moment, and we don't have her."

Tristan blew out the breath he'd been holding. "Where?"

"Outside an airport in Rome. She popped up on facial recognition."

"Did she board a plane?"

Noah raked a hand through his mop of dirty-blond curls, clearly frustrated that they hadn't been able to detain her. "We don't know. Not under her own name, of course, but we're combing through footage from the airport and surrounding area, with a special focus on transportation hubs."

"You think she's coming back home." It wasn't a question.

"That's the current theory. We were able to retrieve the operative you killed at the waterfall, and he's been positively identified as a higher-up in her organization."

"What about the two I ran into on the mountain?"

He was already shaking his head. "In the wind, if they made it off the mountain."

"You think she's coming back to handle things herself?"

"That's the working theory."

"Okay. Good. That's good. Maybe we'll be able to get her this time." A glimmer of hope flared.

"From your mouth to God's ear."

"Yes, sir." Tristan ran a hand over the scratchy stubble he hadn't taken time to shave after receiving Avery's frantic message. "And Mitch?"

"My guess? Lower level. Probably doesn't know much."

"From what I saw in the cave, his partner was the one in contact with Rossi. Mitch was just following orders." Still, he needed to hear what the guy had to say. "I want in on the interview anyway."

Noah studied him, pursed his lips, then finally nodded. "But keep yourself under control."

Tristan started to bristle. But Noah was right. He was taking a chance letting Tristan in on the interview. If he conducted himself in an unprofessional manner, he could blow their whole case. Any good defense lawyer would be able to get him off, and Gianna's attorneys were some of the best in the business. No way would he risk letting the man who'd kidnapped Lily and terrorized Avery walk away. "Got it."

Noah tilted his head and lifted a brow.

Tristan put his palms up. "It won't be a problem."

"All righty, then, let's have at it." They strolled toward the interview room, with Storm at Tristan's side, taking their time since it would take a few minutes for Oliver to get Mitch fingerprinted and processed and hopefully identified. Though Tristan suspected Noah was right. If their interaction in the cave was any indication, Mitch wasn't very high up on the food chain. "He ask for a lawyer yet?"

"Nah. He's probably still trying to figure out who he's more scared of—us or Rossi. I noticed you haven't asked about Avery and Lily," Noah said casually.

Tristan stopped short, glared at him, the sudden change of subject catching him off guard. "Are they okay?"

"They are. We've set up a makeshift infirmary upstairs, so we could keep them close. Dr. Keller is with them. If you want, you could go by and check in on them before we talk to Mitch. You need to get checked out anyway. We can hold off the interview for a bit."

Tristan considered the offer, but he still wasn't sure where he stood with Avery, though he knew exactly where he stood with Lily. She was terrified of him. It was probably best to give her a little space to get used to him before approaching her again. "Let's get this done with before Mitch decides he's more scared of Rossi and requests an attorney."

"If he contacts her, it might give us a chance to find her."

Huh. Maybe. Still… "Let's see what we can get from him first."

Noah nodded then studied him. "Sounds like a plan. But you're going to have to face Avery and Lily sooner or later. You do know that, right?"

Yeah. No kidding. And hopefully by then he'd have answers for them. "I know."

Noah preceded him, then opened the interview room door and held it for Tristan. "You know Storm has to wait here."

He did, lest Mitch try to claim they'd used the big dog that had already attacked him in the woods to intimidate or coerce information out of him. Even though his partner usually went everywhere with him, this was one adventure the Newfie would have to sit out. "Storm, sit."

"Last chance to observe instead," Noah offered—a little too hopefully, in Tristan's opinion.

"I'm good." He paused, then faced Noah directly. "But thank you for this."

"You bet."

Oliver led Mitch in a moment later and cuffed him to the table, not that there was anywhere to go in the highly unpopulated area, even if he did manage to escape the room and somehow make it out of the building where a hundred or so armed FBI employees worked. He then handed Noah and Tristan each a folder.

When Noah leaned his back against a wall to peruse the information they'd been able to amass in only a few minutes, Tristan took a seat at the table across from Mitch and opened his own folder. Mitchell Sullivan had a rap sheet a mile long, though mostly for misdemeanor thefts and a few assaults. He'd sat in jail a few times awaiting trial and done one three-year stint in prison, where it seemed he'd met up with his co-conspirator from the cave, whose body had been recovered from the river and positively identified. Since then, his record was clean, probably thanks to Gianna Rossi's tutelage.

The instant their attorney entered the room, Tristan nodded to him, closed the folder and stared Mitch down. "You are aware kidnapping is a federal offense?"

His eyes widened. "We didn't take her out of the state."

Try as he might, Tristan wasn't able to pull off the casual shrug he'd aimed for.

Noah cleared his throat.

Tristan worked to relax his posture. "Doesn't matter. You kidnapped the child of a federal agent in order to coerce him into refusing to testify. Federal offense, punishable by life in prison."

Mitch slammed his cuffed hands against the steel tabletop and surged to his feet. "You can't put me in jail for life, dude."

Bile surged up the back of Tristan's throat, leaving a sour taste in his mouth—or perhaps that taste came from the deal the government attorney had already approved, which he knew he was going to have to offer.

Seeming to sense his discomfort, Oliver took over, ever the voice of calm reason. "Of course, if you had something to offer in exchange, we might be able to help you out. You'd still go to prison, but you might get out before you die."

"No way, man. I want…" He frowned, tried to reach up, but the chain caught his hands. "You know, that thing where I walk away. No prison. I want that."

"Immunity?" Oliver lifted a brow.

Noah crossed one ankle over the other where he still stood against the wall and let out a low chuckle. "That is not happening, *man*."

"And I want protection. I won't say a word unless you give me protection." Mitch flopped back onto the chair and lowered his head so he could scratch his temple with his cuffed hands. Then he turned his attention to the attorney, probably hoping he was the most compassionate guy in the room. But he'd be mistaken. Tristan had worked with Timothy Bradley before, and the man could be ruthless. "There isn't a prison in the country that woman and her husband can't get to me in."

Wait. What? Tristan looked over his shoulder at Noah and narrowed his eyes.

Noah's casual pose didn't change a bit, yet Tristan could tell he'd gone on alert. It seemed he hadn't heard about the nuptials, either.

"Husband?" Tristan asked, his tone neutral despite the adrenaline spike.

"Yeah, that maniac she married last year. Guy's off his rocker, if you ask me. He's even meaner and more sinister…than…" He trailed off as he lifted his gaze to Tristan, then shifted between Noah and Oliver and seemed to realize the value of the information he was sharing. "He's worse even than she is, and that ain't easy, 'cause she's as coldhearted as they come. And I can give him to you, give them both to you, but only if I get immunity. That's the deal. Take it or leave it."

Leaving Mitch with the attorney, Noah walked out and held the door for two agents stationed in the hallway to enter and Tristan and Oliver to emerge.

Storm immediately trotted to Tristan's side.

Tristan widened his stance and planted his hands on his hips, fully ready for the coming battle. "No. No way."

Noah held up his hands as if in surrender. "I'm not saying—"

"That man kidnapped a child—my child!" Tristan seethed. "No way does he walk. Not happening."

"I'm with Tristan on this one, boss." Oliver stood firm. "No immunity."

Tristan offered him a silent thank-you. He'd owe him for having his back on this. Because there was absolutely no chance he was going to Avery and telling her Lily's kidnapper had gone free because he possessed valuable intel that they wanted.

"Agreed," Noah placated. "Not immunity, but maybe reduced charges in exchange for information that leads directly to the arrest of Gianna Rossi or her supposed husband. Let Tim talk to him, see what intel he actually has and determine its worth, then we'll see what's what.

You know Tim will discuss it with us before making a final determination, considering it was your daughter that was taken. And he's not known for making soft deals."

That was true. Tim Bradley hated letting criminals walk free, and he'd try to get as much information as he could while offering the least leniency in return.

"Just think about it," Noah said.

Tristan would do no such thing, but he was saved from having to argue further when Noah's phone signaled an incoming text.

He fished it out of his pocket, read the new message. "All right. I have to go take care of this, but we'll meet back here in an hour. Tristan, you go talk to Avery, check in on Lily and take a few minutes to calm down so we can all think clearly. In the meantime, I'll get Val on finding out what she can about Rossi's supposed groom. If we can get the intel any other way, a deal will be off the table."

Knowing it was the best he was going to get, Tristan nodded and raked a hand through his hair. "Yeah, boss. Okay."

Noah gestured for Oliver to go with Tristan, then turned and headed for the elevator.

"I don't need a babysitter."

"Maybe not…" Oliver shot him a grin. "But I bet you could use a friend."

He scrubbed his hands over his face. What he needed was for time to stand still for just a second so he could get his bearings. "Yeah, that I could use."

"Come on, then." He clapped Tristan on the back and started for the stairwell at the end of the corridor. "Why don't you introduce me to that little girl of yours?"

Storm fell into step with them.

"Yeah, man, about that…" Tristan started, unsure how

to broach the subject of Lily. The poor kid must be terrified after what she'd been through. He would find out from Dr. Keller how she was doing then figure out what she needed and make sure she had it. "If you wouldn't mind—"

An explosion shook the building, knocking him against the wall.

"It came from the front of the building." Oliver was already moving in that direction.

Tristan overtook him with Storm racing beside him. He shoved through the door to the stairwell. He never should have left Avery and Lily.

SEVEN

Avery's first instinct when she heard the boom of the explosion was to take Lily and run, but Bella hit a button that slammed the doors shut and had an alarm blaring.

Then she stood in front of the door practically vibrating with energy.

A feeling Avery knew all too well. "We can't stay here."

"Yes. We can, and we will, until help comes." She crossed the small makeshift infirmary and laid a hand on Avery's shoulder. "It's the safest place right now. We have no idea what happened yet. It could be something totally unrelated."

"You don't believe that."

Bella sent her a wry smile. "Not for a minute, but it could also be a diversion to flush you outside and give your adversaries a clearer target."

Right. She hadn't thought of that. Where was Tristan? Had he been injured in whatever had just exploded? The sound had sent shock waves reverberating through the building, and Avery was sure she smelled smoke. Though she had to concede, that odor could well be coming from her and Lily's clothing.

Lily, still groggy from the sedative the doctor had given

her so he could tend to her injuries, kept her hands pressed against her ears and stared wide-eyed at Avery.

Knowing there was nothing she could do at the moment, whether she liked it or not, she went to Lily, gathered her off the stretcher into her arms and rocked her. “Shh, baby. It’s okay. Mama’s here. It’s just an alarm to call the firefighters. Nothing to be afraid of.”

Great. Now she was lying to her daughter, something she’d sworn she’d never do. But what other choice did she have? Tell her the truth, that they were in the crosshairs of some deranged killer? And that Rossi might once again be coming for her? No way. She’d already been frightened enough.

“Avery.” Dr. Keller, an older man with short silver hair, kind blue eyes and the build of a linebacker spoke softly and slid a hard-backed chair toward her. “Why don’t you sit down here with Lily on your lap so I can finish treating her?”

“Right. Yes.” She’d need to keep Lily still so the doctor could finish patching up her scrapes and bruises. “Sorry.”

“You have nothing to be sorry for.” He laid a gentle hand on her shoulder, his commanding presence a comfort. “We all have our jobs to do. Yours is to tend to Lily, and mine is to finish with this wound.”

“Of course.” She nodded and adjusted the oxygen mask being used to treat Lily for smoke inhalation. Lily had shifted it when the alarms started going. “You’re right.”

“And the others will take care of whatever is going on out there.” His smile brought a sparkle to his eyes as he took a moment to move her own oxygen tube back into place beneath her nose and pat her shoulder reassuringly. “But I’d like to get you two cleaned up as quickly as possible in case we do have to move.”

She shifted Lily so she straddled her lap, then rubbed circles on her lower back until she hugged her blanket and snuggled her head against Avery's chest.

"There's a good girl," Dr. Keller soothed. "You are doing a fantastic job, Lily. You're a very brave girl. Did you know that?"

Lily nodded groggily against Avery's shoulder.

Avery was grateful for the doctor's constant monologue as he cleaned and bandaged Lily's various injuries. Not only did it soothe Lily and keep her at ease, it allowed Avery a minute to take a breath and try to clear her mind. Unfortunately, clarity didn't bring answers. She had no idea what she was supposed to do next. Where would they go? Her house might well have gone up in the fire. And even if it hadn't, it wasn't safe to return there, not as long as whoever was gunning for them was still on the loose.

And even if they caught all the gunmen and eliminated the threat, she'd have a massive cleanup ahead of her if she could return home. Everything in the house would no doubt reek from smoke. The broken glass would have to be cleaned up and the windows replaced. This wasn't helping to calm her. If anything, it was increasing her tension. She shifted uncomfortably.

"Unbelievable," Dr. Keller muttered under his breath and frowned down at Lily's shoulder.

"Sorry. I didn't mean to move," Avery said.

"Oh, no, dear, it's not that. It's just these bruises, as if someone grabbed her. I'd like to ice them, but is it okay if I remove her locket?"

"Locket?"

The doctor lifted a small, silver locket hung on a long chain around Lily's neck.

Panic surged through Avery. "That's not hers."

"Oh?"

She couldn't take the thought of anything those men had touched still clinging to her daughter. "Get it off her. Now. Please."

Dr. Keller removed the locket and set it aside, then placed an ice pack against Lily's shoulder.

She flinched and snuggled closer to Avery, who had to once again reposition Lily's oxygen mask.

"There, that should make you feel better, little one." Dr. Keller smiled kindly, eliciting a hesitant smile from Lily in return. "Just keep—"

The door burst open and Tristan, with Storm at his side, and the other agent he'd been with—Oliver, she thought—strode through, weapons drawn.

Oliver took up a position flanking the door opposite Bella.

Tristan rushed straight to Avery and Lily. "Are you guys okay?"

"That's the dog that saved me." Lily reached out for Storm.

Storm went straight to her and sat at her side, his gaze firmly on the door. When Lily gripped the fur on his head, he leaned into her without losing his focus.

Fighting back tears of relief that threatened the instant she'd spotted Tristan, Avery nodded. She'd have to examine her reaction more closely later, when she was in a better frame of mind, or maybe never. Because she had no idea if that relief came from the fact that he was unharmed or the fact that he'd come to help them. Either way, she was allowing him to get too close. "What happened?"

He looked down to find Lily's big blue eyes, so much like his own, open and fixed on him.

His radio crackled to life, saving him from having to

find some convoluted way to explain, without frightening Lily, that someone had attacked the building. "Yeah," Tristan said into the radio.

"Do you have them?" came Noah's voice.

"Yes, sir. Everyone here is safe and accounted for."

"We need to talk."

"Be right there." He started for the door.

Avery reached out and grabbed his hand before she could catch herself. "You're leaving?"

Lily's gaze dropped to their joined hands. At least, her experience so far hadn't seemed to dull her curiosity, or her uncanny ability to notice everything that went on around her. A trait she must have inherited from her father. When they were young, Tristan could walk into a room and tell you pretty much everything about it within seconds.

Avery quickly released his hand. "Sorry."

A pained expression crossed his features, but only for an instant before his carefully neutral countenance returned. "I'm just going to step over by the door to speak to my boss. I'm not going anywhere. I won't leave you and Lily in danger, Avery. I promise you that."

When the door opened next, a burly man with a mop of curly blond hair who she assumed was Noah stepped inside. He and Tristan spoke in hushed tones, no doubt in deference to Lily's presence, and Avery had to strain to hear the muted conversation.

Noah glanced over at them and gave a curt nod before turning his full attention to Tristan and the other two agents. "We don't think they were the intended targets."

Tristan frowned. "The explosion was a distraction?"

"We believe so."

"For what purpose?" Oliver asked.

"They set off a car bomb out front to draw us all to Avery and Lily." He swiped a hand over his mouth, his anger palpable in the small space. "In the meantime, they breached the side door, took out Tim Bradley, three of our guards, and eliminated the witness."

Tristan jerked as if he'd been slapped. "Oh, man. Tim?"

Noah nodded.

Tristan slumped, silent for a moment, then massaged his temples as if to ward off a headache. His voice rose, filled with emotion. "How did they even get in?"

"As best we can figure, they had an inside guy. We have Tim and the two guards who were in the room with him as well as the guy stationed outside the door down, and one guard missing."

Oliver scratched his head. "You think the missing guy's a mole?"

Noah nodded. "Caught him on camera going out the back door after the shooting, along with another man we've yet to identify."

"Another guy who works for us?" Bella asked.

"He was wearing an FBI jacket, but we can't be sure. We've done a head count and no one else is unaccounted for at the moment."

"All right. Okay." Tristan raked a hand through his already tousled hair and shifted his gaze to Avery and Lily. "You think that's how they found him so quickly?"

"Actually—" Dr. Keller held up a pair of tweezers with a small metal square caught between them. "I think I can explain that."

Tristan frowned. "What is that?"

Dr. Keller set the tweezers down on a tray and held up the locket he'd taken from Lily's neck. "If I'm not mistaken, it's a tracking device."

Tristan and Noah both approached, propped their hands on their hips and stared down at the tiny device as if it might jump up and either attack or provide answers. Neither of which happened, yet neither man seemed to question the doctor's assessment. Nor did either of them make any attempt to question Lily, which Avery truly appreciated.

But anger simmered just below the surface, not the strong surge of rage that had come earlier, but the kind that lingered and festered over time. She'd suffered with anger like that before, when she'd found out she was pregnant and realized Tristan wasn't coming back and her grandfather's condition was only worsening. When she'd thought she was on her own, anger had settled in her then.

Then, one day, while she sat on the smooth, hard surface of a boulder beside the very same waterfall they'd rescued Lily from, with the sun beating down on her, cocooning her in its warm embrace, she'd realized she wasn't alone. God was with her, had always been with her. It was she who'd turned away. And when she'd returned to the faith her grandfather had instilled in her when she was little, God had welcomed her with open arms, despite the mistakes she'd made. And she was finally able to let that anger go, to find it in her heart to forgive Tristan for breaking his promises. And God had blessed her with the most amazing gift in the world.

She hugged Lily tighter, letting love pour through her and shove the anger aside. She wouldn't live that way, refused to live with a heart full of hatred, bitterness and rage. Then, as she returned her focus to the conversation at hand, something in her settled and she once again found peace.

Noah had lifted the tweezers and was turning the

miniscule device this way and that while he examined it closely. "I wasn't even aware this technology existed. Something this small with a long enough range for Rossi's men to find her."

Oliver and Bella had apparently joined them while Avery had been lost in thought. And since it seemed Lily had fallen asleep, if her soft steady breaths and limp body were any indication, no one seemed too concerned with speaking quietly any longer.

Oliver squinted and leaned closer. "It doesn't. At least, not for practical use. Maybe in testing."

Bella blew out a frustrated breath. "What kind of resources does this woman have?"

"Endless," Tristan said softly, shoulders slumped.

Noah reached out to him, more friend than boss as far as Avery could tell, and clapped a hand on his back. "Not endless, Tristan. And she's not infallible. She already messed up once getting caught on camera in Rome, because she's impatient. Remember when you first came out of your assignment with her organization and you told us that was how we were going to catch her? You insisted she was too impatient for her own good, and that is still true."

"Yeah." He nodded, inhaled deeply and blew the breath out slowly. "You're right."

"Don't worry." Oliver lifted a fist. "We've got this, bro."

Tristan gave his fist a bump, and his posture straightened, as if the show of solidarity had lent him strength. "So, what's next?"

Noah released him, stuffed his hands into his pockets and rocked back onto his heels. "You tell us. You know her better than anyone, were able to get closer to her than anyone else has. And I want justice, Tristan, not only for what she's done to all those families, and what she's done to your family..."

Avery stiffened at the term.

But for Tim Bradley, who I considered a friend, as well as the three guards she eliminated without a care in the world to make sure Mitch would never have the chance to provide us information or testify against her.

As Avery realized the implication—that Tristan was also a witness set to testify against this woman—she gasped. Feelings she didn't understand coursed through her. Fear for her daughter, and even for her own life, were certainly understandable. But it was the terror that gripped her at the thought of anything happening to Tristan that had her so confused.

From what she'd seen, he'd made a good life for himself. He obviously had close people he cared about, who also cared about him. He'd taken over Storm's training and become his handler when Gianna Rossi had presumably killed his friend. So, why hadn't he ever come back? Pain she'd thought long settled prickled. He was clearly still capable of love—perhaps just not for her.

But he'd told her, hadn't he? He'd said he couldn't return after his parents were killed because anyone he met could be their killer. Could she understand that? Could she sympathize with his fears? Yes, she could at least sympathize. She couldn't imagine the pain he'd suffered when his parents had been murdered, the sense of helplessness when the sheriff proved unable to bring their killer to justice. And, with the daunting thought of returning to Timberwood Falls, knowing anyone she ran into on the street could be one of Gianna Rossi's operatives out to get her or Lily, sympathy blossomed from a soft niggle somewhere deep inside her to full blown understanding.

With the realization came the certainty that she'd have to work with Tristan to co-parent Lily in the future, if that's what he wanted. Tristan might not be able to return to Timberwood Falls, but Avery would. It was her home, and Lily would need the familiar surroundings to help her heal. But she could meet up with Tristan elsewhere for him to spend time with his daughter. She might not be willing or able to let him back into her own heart, to risk the pain of falling in love and then losing him again, but he'd already proven he would do anything for Lily.

She hoped he would want a relationship with his daughter. Avery had grown up without her own parents, and she didn't want that for Lily. Her little girl deserved to have her mother and her father in her life, loving her, caring for her, protecting her. As Tristan's parents had done for him, and her grandfather had done for her. The pain of losing him came fast and hard.

Then another thought occurred, robbing her of breath. How could she risk leaving Lily all alone in the world? She couldn't.

"Tristan." She looked up to find all eyes on her, and heat flared in her cheeks. "I'm sorry. I…uh…need to talk to you about something. It's important."

"Sure."

"We'll leave you guys alone for a minute. I'll let you know as soon as we're ready to move." Noah kept the tweezers pinched between his fingers as he left.

"Move where? Are we leaving here?" Not that they were safe there, considering there had already been an explosion and five murders in the short span of time since they'd arrived, but having all the agents surrounding them, at least, offered the illusion of safety.

"Yeah." Tristan closed his eyes and massaged the

bridge of his nose between his thumb and forefinger, exhaustion clearly beating at him. "We'll take you and Lily to a safe house."

"You're coming?"

"Yes. Storm and I will be with you until Gianna Rossi is caught and put in prison." His jaw clenched tight while he waited for Dr. Keller to finish up.

The doc finished taping a bandage over an abrasion on Lily's arm, smoothed her hair in an affectionate gesture, then gritted his teeth for an instant before regaining his composure and stepping back. He held out an oxygen tube for Tristan. "I'll give you two a minute as long as you put that under your nose to treat the smoke inhalation while you chat. But let me know as soon as you're done, Tristan, so I can stitch up Avery's temple and let her and Lily get cleaned up then tend to the rest of your wounds."

He frowned. "Is it okay to wait to stitch Avery?"

"She'll be fine for a few minutes. I have a feeling whatever she needs to talk to you about is probably more important at the moment." He squeezed Avery's shoulder and gave her a stern look. "But don't take too long."

She couldn't help but smile. "Thanks, Dr. Keller."

"You bet." With that, he winked and walked out with Oliver and Bella, who remained just outside the door where she could see them through the glass.

Avery stilled for a minute to be sure Lily really was sleeping, then blew out a breath she hadn't realized she was holding. Was she sure about what she was about to ask him? No, not at all, but what other choice did she have?

Tristan leaned his back against the stretcher, crossed one ankle over the other and folded his arms over his chest. "What's up?"

She took a deep, shaky breath and prayed she was making the right choice. “I need to talk to you about Lily.”

He lurched upright. “Is she okay? The doc said everything was all right, but I could tell he seemed angry. Is something wrong?”

“No, no. It’s not that. I think he was just angry about what was done to her.” She swiped her hair out of her face so she could face him directly, gauge his reaction. This was more difficult than she’d expected, and she choked up the first time she tried to ask, then had to take a deep breath and try again. “If anything happens to me—”

“No. We are not having this conversation. Nothing is going to happen to you.”

“You can’t promise that, Tristan.” She lowered her gaze to Lily’s tangled blond hair. “No one knows the future.”

“I know I won’t let anyone near you. I’ll stand between you and whatever danger comes your way.” He reached for her, lifted her chin until she had no choice but to look into his eyes, to believe the sincerity she found there. “The only way anyone is getting to you or Lily is if they go through me.”

Warmth spread through her, but it couldn’t deter her from what needed to be said. “Thank you, and I appreciate that more than you’ll ever know. But I need to ask you. Um… We haven’t had time to discuss how you feel about staying in Lily’s life once this is all over.”

His jaw tightened.

“Please don’t take this wrong, I’m not pressuring you. It’s just…”

“Hey.”

She paused, held her breath, waited.

“I hope it’s okay with you, but I have every intention of being a part of Lily’s life. She’s my…” He swallowed hard, took a moment to compose himself. "She's my daughter, and I want to be a father to her. I can't help what's happened so far, but I don't want to miss any other part of her life. Moving forward, I will be here for her always."

She sobbed, unable to take the thought of leaving Lily, yet knowing it was a possibility. Truthfully, it had been a concern even before all of this, had intruded on her thoughts every now and again since her grandfather had passed away. She had no other family. No close friends, since she'd pulled away from everyone when Tristan had left and she'd found out she was pregnant. For the past several years, she'd been juggling raising her child and being her grandfather's primary caretaker. Even though she had casual friends, attended church and community functions, she'd never allowed anyone too close. She'd never been able to open up to anyone, never been able to trust.

And now she was faced with having to trust someone, the same someone who'd betrayed her in the first place, with the most important thing in the world. "If anything happens to me, I need you to promise me you'll take care of Lily."

"Avery…" Tristan's voice was no more than a hoarse croak.

Pain squeezed her chest, radiated through her limbs. Could she really trust him with this? With Lily? She needed to make him understand the trust she was placing in him, but she couldn't force the words past the lump clogging her throat. So, she said all she could manage. "Please, Tristan. I need you to promise me that."

He cradled her cheek, his hand warm against her face.

She tilted into his touch. She'd been strong for so long, but she would allow herself this one moment of comfort.

A tear tipped over his lashes and rolled down his cheek. Then he leaned forward, pressed his forehead against hers and whispered, "I promise."

Tristan switched on his high beams to push back some of the darkness enveloping the mountain road. Thick cloud cover filled him with a sense of claustrophobia and dread as he drove the Suburban toward the safe house. Avery was safely riding shotgun, Lily snored softly from the car seat behind them and Storm was comfortably secured in the cargo hold. Oliver and Bella followed in another SUV, lingering just far enough back to intervene if another attack came.

While at the safe house, Lily and Avery would be protected by the Timberwood Falls sheriff and his deputies. And the thought rankled. Not an ideal situation, from his point of view anyway, but necessity won out over his comfort. And with their FBI office compromised, there were only a handful of agents Noah and Tristan both completely trusted. Oliver and Bella had come with him, since they'd agreed a female agent should remain in the same room with Avery and Lily at all times to assure the highest level of protection, and Cayden had agreed to stay with Noah to find out how Gianna Rossi had managed to infiltrate their unit and root out any agents whose loyalty might still lie with her. A daunting task, considering they had to check finances in case Rossi had paid someone off and conduct background searches in case there were past connections they'd missed.

The betrayal piqued his anger all over again, and he tightened his grip on the wheel as he navigated the switchbacks and inclines.

"You okay?" Avery asked softly, the first words she'd uttered since leaving the FBI building.

He spared her a glance. She looked tired, circles ringing her eyes. Even after getting cleaned up, her hair hung limp, with none of its usual luster. "I'm fine."

Avery gestured toward the steering wheel and offered a wry half smile. "You might want to ease up a bit before you crack that in half."

Tristan couldn't help but chuckle, which relaxed his muscles, including those holding the wheel in a death grip. He rolled his shoulders, tilted his head from side to side to ease the tension in his neck and tried to relax his posture. What had him wound so tight? The attack on their headquarters and the agents they'd lost—definitely. But there was more. So much more.

He was not looking forward to working with Sheriff Reynolds again. In the five years since his parents' murders, the man had done nothing to move their case forward. Each and every call for information Tristan had made over the years had been met with a callous "Sorry, but we have no new leads."

Even after Tristan had joined the FBI, Reynolds had offered nothing. He'd never once indicated he'd found a suspect, had supposedly recovered not one shred of physical evidence to connect anyone to his parents' murders and hadn't offered information on a single lead in five years. As far as he could tell, Reynolds had basically accepted that the case had gone cold right from the start.

And now they had to depend on the very same man to make arrangements to keep Avery and Lily protected. Since they couldn't trust the information wouldn't leak from their FBI office, they'd reached out to local law enforcement in Timberwood Falls to set up a safe house and provide a few additional officers for protection. Tristan had argued in favor of taking them halfway around the world to some remote destination, but Noah, Oliver and Cayden had all argued against it. They'd reminded him Rossi had last been spotted in Rome.

So, was there anywhere truly safe? Probably not. At least in Timberwood Falls they had local law enforcement they knew, plus, Cayden and Noah could reach them by chopper in no time if the need arose. Besides, it was probably a move Rossi wouldn't expect. And, the clincher for Tristan, Lily might be more comfortable in familiar surroundings.

She'd been so quiet. And beating himself up over the fact that he didn't know if that was normal for her didn't help matters. If anything, it made things worse. He couldn't think about that now, though. He needed to keep his focus on saving them. Any thought of knowing Lily better would have to come later. He shoved his emotions into a box and buried it deep, then took a calming breath, concentrated on the hypnotic hum of the tires against pavement and forced his thoughts back to Sheriff Reynolds.

He lost his hard-won battle to ease his tension as the thought of the man ratcheted his anxiety right back through the roof again. In all fairness, though, it was easier to cling to anger at Reynolds than to accept defeat. The outcome of his parents' case might not be the sheriff's fault. Sometimes, despite hard work and the best of intentions, the bad guys got away. Thus explaining his current situation. If Tristan hadn't let her get away, Gianna Rossi would be behind bars right now instead of terrorizing his family.

His family. The thought brought him up short, as it

had the first time Oliver had uttered the phrase. Although this time the concept didn't seem quite as foreign. Had he grown more comfortable with the sentiment since then? Was that what Avery and Lily were to him now—how he viewed them? He couldn't deny his feelings for Avery. Being away from her over the years had been difficult, but it was nothing in comparison to being with her again.

If anything, his feelings for her may have become stronger. She'd changed in the time he'd been gone. She'd grown stronger and more confident. Instead of becoming bitter and angry at her losses, she'd come to appreciate her blessings even more. And yet, none of her kindness had been diminished. She was no longer the sweet, naïve girl he'd loved, but a courageous, compassionate, loving woman. And she'd instilled those same qualities in their daughter.

Lily… What could he even say about his little girl? She'd yet to speak a word to him, had eyeballed him like he was a perp and she an interrogator, and yet… The thought had a smile tugging at him. Maybe there was some of him in her after all. Until that moment, she'd seemed all Avery, strong, kind, beautiful… Except for her eyes, the same big blue eyes that would stare back at him if he moved his gaze to the rearview mirror. He shifted again, uncomfortable with the new path his thoughts had headed down. Why couldn't he keep Avery and Lily off his mind?

It wasn't lost on him that Avery had trusted him enough to ask him to take Lily, though the thought of anything happening to Avery sucked the breath from his lungs leaving nothing but an empty, hollow pit. Nor was it lost that he'd been too choked up to offer her anything more than the simple promise that he would.

What he'd wanted to do was reassure her that he would love their child and care for her if the need arose, but the mind-numbing pain at the thought of Avery being killed had robbed him of breath, and apparently speech, since he'd only nodded and muttered a muffled "I promise" before turning and walking away to find a space where he could break down for just a few minutes in private.

"You know, you might try praying." Her words broke the heavy silence, startling him.

"Huh?"

She gestured toward the steering wheel, where his hands had, seemingly of their own accord, once again resumed their death grip. "When I'm stressed, I find praying helps. It relaxes me, brings me a sort of peace that allows me to think more clearly."

Tristan shrugged, uncomfortable with the topic, but at least she was speaking to him, and maybe he owed her honesty if nothing else. He'd grown up going to mass with his parents every Sunday, then going out for brunch afterward. Them and about half of Timberwood Falls. He smiled at the memory of the few times Avery had accompanied his family. Then, when he'd become a teenager, he'd still held on to his faith, but he'd strayed, wrapped up with school and sports, and he'd started skipping Church. Longing for that special time with his parents filled him, a dull ache he had no hope of relieving. If only he could go back. "My relationship with God…uh…fractured, I guess, a long time ago."

She frowned. "I don't understand."

He maintained eye contact for a second or two, as long as possible on the dark, winding road, searching to see if she truly was interested in his answer. Once he was convinced she was simply curious and not passing judgment, he resigned himself to the uncomfortable truths he was about to face. “The first time I’ve prayed in years was when I found out about Lily and that she’d been taken. I didn’t know what else to do. I wouldn’t have been a hypocrite and prayed for myself, but I prayed for her.”

“Prayer has become my first response rather than my last resort, though it’s often that, too.”

“Either way, I’m pretty sure God gave up on me.” And he was surprised to find the idea brought a stab of pain to his heart.

Her soft laughter wasn’t what he’d expected. “God doesn’t give up on us, Tristan. We’re the ones who turn away from Him.”

“Yeah, well.” He swallowed hard, forcing what felt like paste down his throat.

“There was a time, after you left…” She turned to gaze out the window, watching the miles pass, and he thought she might have decided to let things drop.

Who knew? Maybe that was for the best.

Then she spoke again, softly, without turning her gaze from the landscape. “I was so lost, Tristan. I didn’t know what to do or where to turn. My grandfather had cancer and needed constant care, I’d just found out I was pregnant, and the love of my life, the person I’d counted on for so long to stand by my side, was just gone. I was barely twenty-three years old, and my life was a mess.”

The thought weighed him down. He’d failed her. “I’m so sorry, Avery.”

“Hey, no.” She gripped his wrist, waited for him to turn to her, then maintained her hold. “I’m not saying this to make you feel bad. It’s not your fault. I just want you to understand what a dark place I was in. I was scared—more like terrified, exhausted and utterly alone. I didn’t grow up in a religious household like you did, but I was convinced God was punishing me. Then, one day, I was driving past that beautiful old church on the corner of Main Street in town, the one you brought me to with your parents those times when we were young, and it looked so inviting, so comforting, so safe. I could remember the look of joy on your mom's face as she watched me look around and soak it all in that first time as if it were yesterday. And I missed her, terribly. Then, I just had this compulsion to be inside those ancient stone walls, with the light shining through the stained-glass windows falling over me. And before I knew it, I'd parked in the lot and was walking inside."

When she paused, he simply waited her out, giving her a moment to compose her thoughts, giving himself a moment to wallow in his regrets.

"The instant I walked in and sat down, it felt like…" She hesitated. "It felt like coming home after a long trip. And there was a priest there. He invited me in, and we sat together, prayed together, talked… When I left there, my problems weren't automatically gone, and my circumstances hadn't changed, but I no longer felt alone. And when I prayed, more and more regularly as time went on, even if just a 'Thank You, God, for this day, for this child' or a 'Please, let Tristan be safe out there somewhere,' it brought me a sense of peace that had eluded me before that."

She'd prayed for him? Even after he'd walked away and left her alone with an ailing grandfather and a baby to care for? When a glimmer of hope that he might one day return fully to his faith started to surface, for the first time in a long time, he didn't tamp it down.

"God forgives us. If we're truly sorry for our sins,

God forgives us and welcomes us home with open arms. Not only does He accept us, He wants us to find our way back to Him."

"My sins are…" How could he explain to her the depth of what he'd done? The things he'd been responsible for? "Many and great."

"You're a good man, Tristan." She released his wrist, leaving him cold and empty. And, like she'd said, alone.

"Would a good man stand by and watch a man be executed?"

She gasped.

"I stood in a room with a man I'd known for the two years I'd been undercover, a man I'd worked alongside, even if that work was illegal and, at a minimum, morally gray. Not that I ever hurt anyone, or kidnapped a child, and when I did find out about any kidnappings, I sent word to Noah and he was able to rescue the children. I never would have done that, would have blown my cover before allowing a child to be harmed." He paused, stared into her eyes, willing her to understand that before he continued.

"I know that, Tristan."

He stared straight ahead at the road in front of him, forcing back the wave of emotions threatening to drown him. The rest of the words tumbled out before he could censor them. "Rossi found out there was a mole in her organization. I don't know how. We'd been so careful. For two years I lived the life of a criminal, no contact with anyone from the outside world other than coded messages to Noah when something needed to be stopped. But she knew. Somehow, she knew. And she called us all to that room, even all of her lower-level operatives who were even remotely involved in that last kidnapping that Noah intervened in. Most of whom had known nothing about the plan in advance. She asked us who leaked the operation. And when no one answered, she walked up to Jeff Cabot and shot him point-blank."

Grief, guilt, pain and shame washed over him, threatening to choke him.

Avery reached out, pried one of his hands from the wheel and interlaced her fingers with his. Then she rested their joined hands between them, and his heart shattered. "Everything happens for a reason, Tristan, even if we don't always understand that reason. If Rossi hadn't shot Cabot without warning, you'd have intervened and saved him, probably at the cost of your own life. You didn't know. You couldn't know. And it wasn't your fault. As for the things you might have had to do or overlook to save those children, I'm sure you did the best you could under the circumstances, and I'm sure their families are grateful. No one gets through life without making mistakes. We're human, after all…" She offered a small smile. "And not perfect. God knows that, and He forgives us. All we have to do is turn back to Him and ask."

She fell quiet then, perhaps contemplating her own thoughts, or maybe just exhausted.

He welcomed the silence, and the warmth of the hand she hadn't pulled away from his. He needed her in that moment, needed her kindness and support. She hadn't judged him, hadn't seen anything bad in him, had instead simply offered him a light to cling to. And for the first time in a long time, he felt a sense of hope, a sense that all might not be completely lost. And he uttered a simple prayer. *God, forgive me.*

"You're going to make the next right." Avery, so quiet since their talk, pointed ahead of them even though the GPS had already alerted him of the upcoming turn. Perhaps she realized his attention lay elsewhere. Or maybe she still knew him well enough to gauge his level of distraction. "It's going to be a dirt road. About a mile up there will be a clearing with a log cabin in the center."

Tristan already knew the layout, had studied it along with her and committed it to memory the instant Reynolds had sent them the plan. More of a lodge than a cabin, amid a clearing in the middle of a thick forest on the side of a mountain. What could go wrong?

"You're sure returning to Timberwood Falls is the right thing to do?" Avery asked quietly.

Was he sure? Not by a long shot. But it was the best they could come up with in a hurry—even if five years hadn't gotten Reynolds any closer to solving his parents' murders. While he wouldn't burden Avery with all that, he'd also promised himself there would be no more lies between them. He might not be able to offer her much, but he could at least give her honesty. "Under the circumstances, we think it's the safest alternative. For now. But if at any point you are uncomfortable, we'll make other arrangements. And Bella is assigned to you and Lily for the entire time. She'll never leave your side."

She nodded and fell back into her silent contemplation.

It didn't take long to reach the house, and after he parked and let Storm out of the cargo area, he and Oliver took the big dog with them and checked the perimeter while Bella waited with Avery and Lily.

Once satisfied all was as it should be, Tristan opened Avery's door, automatically placing himself between her and any possible locations a sniper might lie in wait. "Do you need help with Lily?"

"I'm good, thanks." She got out, looked around, then

leaned into the back seat and slid Lily out of the car seat and into her arms like a pro.

Tristan reached out and grabbed her elbow to guide her and be sure she gained her footing. And because he needed to reassure himself that she was safe. Or, at least, as safe as they could make her. He leaned his head close to hers and spoke softly. "When we get inside, Bella will take you and Lily to your rooms. She will stay with you there until this is done. No matter what happens, you stay with Bella. Don't trust anyone else. Do you understand?"

She nodded, then caught her lower lip between her teeth and frowned. She hesitated before finally asking, "Where will you be?"

"I'll be close by, and I'll check in on you guys once I'm satisfied with all the arrangements."

She nodded and lowered her gaze. To watch that she didn't trip up the three steps leading to the front porch? Or did he dare hope that was disappointment that he wouldn't be right with her? Either way… "I'll be close by if you need me."

"Thank you, Tristan." She leaned her head against his shoulder.

He wrapped an arm around her in reassurance, wishing they could be walking arm in arm under different circumstances, in a different time and place. His mind wandered down a road to the past, when they'd often strolled through the forest, hands clasped companionably. What would he give to go back to that time, to be that innocent again, to be brimming with love and the promise of the future and unaware of the cruelty the world could bring?

"I'm sorry for all this, Avery." He laid his free hand on Lily's back, felt the rise and fall of her soft breaths. "I'm sorry Lily won't ever know that same sense of innocence and trust we did as kids." A tear slipped out and he turned his head away from her to keep her from noticing.

As they stood on the porch, him shielding those he loved with his body, she turned to him. She shifted Lily's weight and reached up to cradle his cheek, then she gently guided his face back to hers. She wiped the tear that had slipped out with her thumb, then lifted onto her tiptoes and kissed his cheek before stepping back. "None of this is your fault. I understand that now. You were doing what you thought was right, and I have no doubt that if you'd realized we were in danger, you'd have come for us."

The knots in his gut began to unravel.

"That's one of the things I lo… Uh—" She hesitated, stumbled over whatever she'd been about to admit. Or was that just wishful thinking on his part?

"It's one of the things I admire most about you. You always try to do the right thing. And I was wrong for not telling you about Lily earlier, Tristan. And I am so very sorry for that."

He pulled her close, with Lily cradled between them. He couldn't utter the words he wanted to, that he loved her, loved Lily, and would do anything for them. It wasn't the time or the place, and they had to get inside—but he would take this one moment to allow himself to feel the love coursing through him.

Oliver laid a hand on his back. "We need to move, man."

He nodded and guided Avery through the door when Bella opened it, then kept his gaze firmly averted when Bella led her and Lily down the hallway in the direction a sheriff's deputy indicated.

Understanding his role, and knowing Avery and Lily were the first priority, Oliver followed after them.

Tristan closed the door behind them, then turned and found himself face-to-face with the officer in charge of his parents' murder case.

Sheriff Reynolds, a rotund man with slicked-back black hair, now gone gray at the temples, and a 1970s mustache, stood with one hand on his hip, the other on his holstered weapon, and eyed Tristan up and down. "Well, well, well. Look at you, all grown up."

Tristan tried to shake off the nerves the guy elicited and forced himself to extend a hand. He'd forgotten what an egotistical jerk the sheriff could be, but it all came rushing back. The sense of helplessness he'd felt when the sheriff had first knocked on his door and told him his parents had been killed. The condescending attitude each time Tristan had called him for an update on the case. And he was once again that young man, frightened and alone. He shook off the feeling. He was no kid, and he was far from helpless. Plus, now he had an entire team to back him up. And when this was done, he was going to talk to Noah about opening their own investigation into his parents' deaths. It was long past time he found answers. Who knew? Maybe finding answers about his parents might help him to move forward past his grief, be a better father to Lily in the future, even allow him the freedom to come back to town to see her. And Avery. Because the thought of turning and walking away from her again indefinitely filled him with dread. "Sheriff. Thanks for your help with this."

Reynolds shook his hand with a firmer-than-necessary grip, squeezed just a little too long, a bit too hard, then let go. "Don't you worry about a thing. I wanted to be here to make sure you all got in smoothly, but I'll be heading out. My deputies will see to it you have whatever you need."

"Thank you again." And that was that. He refused to ask again about his parents. He wouldn't get answers anyway. So, he didn't even bother to look over his shoulder as Reynolds left, without ever acknowledging Storm, and one of his deputies locked the door behind him. "Come on, Storm."

Tristan made quick work of introducing himself and Storm to the two deputies stationed at the house, jittery with Avery and Lily out of his sight, then strode down the hallway toward his room. Since his door was right across the hall from Avery's, he paused a moment.

Her voice came to him muffled through the closed door. "Come on, Lily. It's time to say your prayers and get into bed."

Before he could talk himself out of it, he lifted a hand and knocked softly. The worst she could do was tell him to go away, right?

"Who is it?" Bella called through the closed door.

"It's me, Bella."

The door swung wide, and she smiled and hooked a thumb over her shoulder. "Come on in, and if you don't mind, I'm going to so see if there's any water bottles in the fridge while you're here."

He knew it was just an excuse to give him a minute alone with Avery and Lily, and he appreciated the gesture. "Thanks, Bella."

"Anytime." She petted Storm's head on her way past.

He waited for her to leave, but then had no idea what to say. He couldn't ever remember being so uncomfortable in Avery's presence, and he didn't like the feeling. They used to talk about everything, from the weather to their deepest emotions. He hadn't realized until just this moment how much he'd missed that camaraderie.

He called to Avery from the doorway. "I…um…" He laid a hand on Storm's head. "*We* just wanted to say good night."

She shoved her hair back out of her face, looking more than a little flustered. "Come on in."

He did as she asked, closing the door behind him, then checking that the heavy curtains were closed over the window. "Everything okay?"

"As okay as it can be, but Lily's overtired and…" She just shook her head. "She doesn't want to go back to sleep."

Lily sat in the middle of the full-size bed, pouting around the thumb that seemed permanently plugged into her mouth, and clutched her blanket against her face. Her eyes widened when she saw Storm, and she dropped the blanket into her lap and opened her arms. "Storm!"

Tristan's breath caught. When Storm looked up at him, he looked to Avery, then released Storm at her nod.

He trotted to the side of the bed.

Still clutching her blanket, which she'd finally allowed them to wash after a prolonged battle while she and Avery had gotten cleaned up before leaving for the safe house, she scooted off the side of the bed and wrapped her arms around Storm's neck.

Avery dropped to her knees, clasped her hands together and propped her elbows on the bed. Then she lowered her forehead onto her hands.

Lily knelt beside her, hands clasped as well, and leaned her head against Storm's side.

Storm sat and rested his big head against hers.

"Now I lay me down to sleep…" Lily started, then looked up at Tristan.

Avery opened her eyes to see why her daughter had stopped mid-prayer.

When Lily reached out a hand to Tristan, his heart hitched and his knees turned to rubber. He went to her, knelt down beside Storm and clasped his trembling hands. He'd veered from his faith for too long, and yet, when he'd asked God for help, He'd answered. It was time to say thank you, time to return to his faith. Too bad it had taken his four-year-old to remind him of that.

Lily smiled at him, then once again closed her eyes. "Now I lay me down to sleep. I pray the Lord my soul to keep. May God guard me through the night, and wake me with the morning light."

She recited the prayer with Avery, but it seemed she knew it well. He could only hope it brought her as much comfort as it brought him. When Avery paused, Lily continued. "God bless Mommy. God bless Tristan. God bless Storm. And please don't let the bad men get us again."

Tristan's heart shattered into a million pieces.

Avery sobbed softly.

Lily snuggled tighter against Storm. "Amen."

EIGHT

Avery lay awake, Lily snoring softly where she'd fallen asleep across her chest, and stared up at the wood beams running along the ceiling. She wrapped her arms tighter around Lily, kissed the top of her head and inhaled deeply, assuring herself her baby was as safe as she could make her.

Storm lifted his head, looked at her and whimpered from his spot at the foot of the bed, where Tristan had let him stay after Lily had begged and before hightailing it out of there without a word once they'd finished their prayers.

"It's all right, boy," Avery whispered, careful not to wake Lily. "I'm sorry I disturbed you."

Lily had slept fitfully, tossing and turning, crying out in her sleep, no doubt harassed by the same nightmares that played out in Avery's mind every time she closed her eyes. How long would it be before she was able to sleep again? To relax? Even Storm's weight against her feet hadn't helped her feel secure. Nor did Bella's presence in the armchair next to the window.

A soft knock on the door startled her, and her heart rate kicked up instantly.

Bella was out of the chair, weapon in hand, before Avery could even blink.

While Bella went to the door, Avery gently shifted Lily off her chest and threw the blanket back. Not fully comfortable with the arrangements, and without knowing if anything would send them on the run again, they'd gone to bed in the leggings and T-shirts Valerie Robinson had provided for them before they'd left for the safe house. Hopefully she wouldn't have to wake Lily from whatever respite she might manage to get.

Bella cracked the door open, peered out, then stepped back and holstered her weapon when Tristan stepped inside, fully dressed, with his holster and shoulder radio in place.

Had he slept at all? Or had he, like she, lain awake contemplating whatever might come next? They needed to talk. She knew that. If this mess ever got resolved. But what would she say? What did she want? Her emotions were all over the place. Could her confusion have added to her insomnia? Probably.

In one way, she wanted to ask him to come home to Timberwood Falls, to be a part of their family. Because she'd already decided this was where she would stay. They still hadn't confirmed the fate of her small house on the mountain, but she had no doubt she wanted to remain in the town she'd grown up in, the only home she'd ever known. It was a wonderful place to raise Lily, and the threat to their lives hadn't come from the small town itself but from outside. She shoved the thoughts away for later as she watched Tristan and Bella whisper softly in the doorway, Tristan's expression tense, Bella's posture stiff. A chill raced through her, and she grabbed a throw from the back of the armchair and wrapped it tightly around herself then sat and waited to see what had Tristan up in the middle of the night. She wished she could open the curtains, stare outside, study the silhouette of the forest as it climbed up the mountainside. Would the view bring comfort? Would the familiarity offer peace of mind? Would it give clarity?

She understood Tristan's reluctance to return home. Murder had chased him away in the first place, and that *had* happened in Timberwood Falls. Plus, he'd made a life for himself as an FBI agent with the Missing Persons Unit, a job he not only seemed to love but was apparently very good at. How many families would depend on him to find their loved ones? Was it selfish for her to wish he'd give all that up to come home to them? Did she even want him to?

She'd come to admire Tristan. Since he'd returned for them, he'd shown nothing but compassion and strength. He was protective and fierce, yet so gentle and patient with Lily. While she still hesitated to open her heart fully to him, especially knowing he was likely to leave when this was all done, she couldn't help some of her reservations beginning to dissipate. She understood him so much better now. Understood his leaving had nothing to do with her or his feelings for her, but with his own struggles, his own fears. She might have forgiven him long ago, but with understanding came a new battle. She just wasn't sure if she was winning or losing that battle as her heart began to open up and trust him again.

Bella's phone signaled a message, and she pulled it out of her pocket and frowned at the screen. "If it's okay, I have to step out for a minute. Oliver wants me."

Tristan nodded. "We're good, Bella, thanks."

She made a beeline down the hallway, leaving Avery

wondering if she'd really been called away or simply wanted to give them some privacy.

Tristan turned the other armchair and sat facing her, then scooted his chair closer until their knees almost touched. He looked over his shoulder and studied Lily for a few moments, then frowned. "Is she doing okay?"

Avery followed his gaze to where Lily lay sleeping, watched as she inhaled and let out a stuttering breath. "I think so. Thank you for letting Storm stay with her. It seemed to help her fall asleep."

"I wanted to talk to you about that."

"About Storm?"

"Well, not exactly." He raked a hand through his hair. "What I mean is, the breeder we got Storm from is expecting another litter, and I'd like to give Lily one of the pups."

"I…uh…" Did that mean he didn't plan on hanging around? Surely, if he did, he wouldn't be asking to gift Lily a puppy of her own since he already had Storm.

"I think it would be good for her, and I spoke to a child psychiatrist we often recommend in kidnapping cases, and she agreed." His words tumbled over each other as if he was in a rush to blurt them all out. "And she's also agreed to see Lily."

"Um…" She struggled to focus, her mind still caught up in thoughts of him leaving. She took a deep breath, let it out slowly.

"That is, if it's okay with you. I mean…" He shoved to his feet, propped his hands on his hips and stared at the curtains as if he could see through them to the mountain beyond. Then he faced her. "Please, say something, Avery. I have no idea where I stand here. I want to do what's right for Lily, but I know I have no right to make decisions about her future."

Some of the fear and doubt started to dissipate. It seemed they were both on shaky ground.

"I know we haven't had much time to talk. Things have been moving at a hundred miles an hour. But I need…" He spread his hands wide, then let them drop to his sides. His shoulders slumped as if he was defeated. "I have no idea what I need."

And just like that, with the realization that he must be just as confused as she was, any lingering fear disappeared, and she gave in to the smile tugging at her. "That makes two of us."

His eyes widened. He blinked a few times. Then he dropped back into the chair.

"You already know I want you to be a part of Lily's life. And of course, you have the right to share in decisions that affect her. I appreciate the fact that her welfare is always the first thing on your mind. So, what do you say we move forward from here as friends? We can work out the logistics of it all once this is done." He propped his elbows on the arms of the chair, clasped his hands together and lowered his head to his hands. A single tear dripped onto his jeans, darkening one spot.

She resisted the urge to reach for him, giving him space to collect himself, while her own emotions raged inside her. Friends? Was that what she wanted? Would that be enough?

Tristan finally looked up and sniffed. "Thank you, Avery."

"I'm just doing what I feel is right, what I should have done five years ago." She knew she had no right to ask, but the words escaped before she could clamp her mouth shut. "Have you ever considered doing anything else besides working with the Missing Persons Unit?"

His gaze met hers then, and the stark honesty she found there gave her the answer she dreaded before he even opened his mouth to answer. "No. This is what I'm meant to do, what I've been called to do. But I promise you, I will find a way to continue my career without putting you or Lily in danger again."

She nodded. Though she wished he could come home and work a danger-free job, she understood his career was a part of who he was now, a part of everything she loved about the man he'd become. "So, now what?"

He took both of Avery's hands in his and rested them on their knees. "I have to go."

"You..." She yanked her hands away, stuffed them beneath her legs. "You what? Why?"

"You can trust Oliver and Bella to keep you and Lily safe, but I have to go finish this."

"But I thought you said..." Said what? That he wouldn't leave them until the danger had passed, that he'd protect them, that he'd stand between Lily and danger at any cost? And now he was leaving them in the hands of others? "Never mind."

"Please, try to understand."

"Understand what? That you sat here and poured your heart out, talked about wanting to remain in Lily's life—" if not in Avery's life "—and now you're just going to walk out? Just like that?"

Lily turned over and whined in her sleep.

Avery reigned in her anger. It was unwarranted, and she knew that. If he didn't arrest Rossi, she and Lily would never be safe. But the thought of him going up against that woman was more than she could take. The image of her shooting him point-blank like she had Cabot was too unbearable to contemplate. She just wished he could stay with them and someone else could go after Rossi. And yet, she already knew he wouldn't turn away from the responsibility, would never put someone else in danger to keep himself safe. And she loved him all the more for it. She lowered her voice. "I'm sorry. You're right. Where is it you have to go?"

"I already told you. I'm going to finish this."

Her heart skipped a beat. "What do you mean, finish it?"

"Noah, Cayden and I worked out a plan. We've planted the locket with the GPS device they used on Lily in a motel room on the outskirts of town. The motel has been emptied except for our operatives, and we believe Gianna Rossi is on her way there."

"Wait, what?" Her gaze shot to Lily. Things were moving too fast for her to keep up. When had this plan been hatched, and why hadn't she been included in it? Then again, why would she be?

"Our facial recognition program picked her up at a small private airport a few hours away." He changed as he spoke, his voice hardening, as any lingering sense of the boy she'd known vanished and the man he'd become, the agent he'd become, took over. "We're going to take her down. Hopefully tonight. The trial for those of her henchmen we were able to apprehend in the original raid begins in a few days, and we plan to have Gianna in custody before that happens."

Avery stood and went to the bottom of the bed. She couldn't just sit there wrestling with the thought of Tristan in danger. She glanced down at Lily.

Tristan came up behind her, wrapped his arms around her waist and rested his chin on her shoulder. How many times had they stood that way? Staring out over the falls, the snow-capped mountains, the wildflower fields? The moment was so tender that for just a second, she could see them together as a family, their lives normal and filled with love rather than fear. Reality intruded too soon, and she turned to face him. "Why do you have to go?"

He smoothed her hair back from her face, tucked the strands behind her ear and caged her eyes with his. "I have to do this, Avery. We have to be careful who we include on the operation after Rossi managed to infiltrate our offices. There just aren't that many agents we can use, and I can't expect my team to go in shorthanded. I won't. Besides, I have to be sure that woman can no longer pose a threat to our daughter."

Our daughter. The words sent a thrill coursing through her.

Then he cradled her face between his hands and, without warning, captured her mouth with his, deepening the kiss until her head swirled, her toes curled and all coherent thought about why this was a bad idea fled. Memories flooded her mind, chasing away everything else. Images from their past played like a biopic behind her closed eyes. And for those few moments she could almost hope they might have the chance to become something more than friends.

Then he pulled away, stepped back, released her, his expression tortured. "I'm sorry, Avery. I don't know what came over me… I… I'm sorry."

She watched him go, Storm trotting beside him, the full implication of his reality hitting her like a physical blow. He had to leave. He'd always have to leave. There would always be another case for him, another operation, another danger. All those she'd lost weighed on her—her parents, her grandfather, Tristan's parents. Could she go through that again? Could she get through the grief of losing him if she opened her heart fully? No. She'd never get past that. How could she ever let herself fall for him again?

Friends. Avery had offered friendship, and what had he done? He'd kissed her. What had he been thinking? How could he have done something like that? And then he'd walked away when there was more, so much more, he'd wanted to say.

Storm shifted in the Suburban's cargo hold, and Tristan glanced in the rearview mirror.

The road behind him was clear. No one had followed him from the safe house. Still, Storm's agitation as he stood, turned around, then settled again against the back seat made him uneasy. Actually, this whole situation gave him pause. Something niggled in his gut, a feeling he'd learned to trust over the years. What was he missing?

Maybe if he wasn't so consumed with thoughts and feelings he had no hope of sorting through, he could wrap his head around what was bothering him with this case. They were on the verge of catching Gianna Rossi. Finally. After two years undercover and another year of searching for the black-market adoption ring's leader, after she'd somehow managed to escape their raid, their efforts were about to pay off. Rossi had kidnapped and sold so many children, only a handful of whom they'd been able to recover thanks to his undercover operation. She'd killed or been responsible for the deaths of numerous FBI agents in both the past raid and most recently at their offices—some of them people he knew, including Benny, who'd been a friend. And if all that wasn't bad enough, which it was, she'd ordered his own child kidnapped and put a hit out on the woman he'd loved with all his heart at one time.

At one time. As if his feelings for Avery were nothing but a distant memory. Yeah, right. And that was probably the biggest lie he'd ever told himself, because if the gut-wrenching fear of losing her was any indication, he'd never stopped loving Avery Taylor. For him, she was the one who got away. Another lie. She was the one he'd up and walked away from. A mistake? Maybe. Probably. Who was he kidding? Absolutely. But what could he do about it now? He couldn't go back and change the past. And he'd made a life for himself, a career that honored his parents, one that mattered, one he loved. One that wasn't conducive to having a family.

Cayden had tried, had given it his best shot despite the demands of the job, and his ex-wife had ended up moving twelve hundred miles away with their infant daughter and her new husband, the man she'd turned to when Cayden had spent too many nights away from home. But was that his fault?

Storm scrambled to his feet and barked, stilled for a minute on full alert, then sat and stared out the back window.

Again, what was he missing? Something. Why did excitement at the thought of capturing Gianna Rossi elude him? And why wouldn't the urge to turn around and go back to Avery and Lily let up? He shifted position, checked the rearview mirror, checked the side-view mirrors, then made a sudden sharp left across the deserted road into a closed strip mall parking lot and headed straight around the back to the staging area Noah had set up.

He wasted no time getting out, releasing Storm and approaching the beat-up-looking, unmarked box truck that housed hundreds of thousands of dollars in surveillance equipment.

The door opened just as he reached it, and Cayden nodded in greeting as Tristan and Storm hurried inside. "No problems?"

He started to blow off the question and simply agree that the short trip from the safe house to the staging area had been uneventful but then had second thoughts. He might not be able to put his finger on what was bothering him, but maybe one of his teammates could, one whose head wasn't cluttered up with emotions.

When he hesitated, Noah looked up from several rows of monitors. "Something happen?"

"No. Not exactly." He stood behind Noah, too agitated to sit, and scanned the monitors showing the outside of the motel where they'd placed the GPS tracking device that Dr. Keller had removed from Lily's locket.

The motel, a dive on the outskirts of Timberwood Falls, had been emptied, its few guests upgraded to a nearby hotel, its staff given the night off with pay. One of Noah's agents, clearly visible from different angles on three of the monitors, leaned back in an office chair behind the front desk with a book in hand and his feet propped on the desk. He reached up to scratch his head and discreetly spoke into a radio that looked like a wristwatch. "Anything?"

The sound of his voice echoed in the metal container.

Noah pressed the button on the radio attached to his shoulder lest he have to move in a hurry. "All clear."

The agent nodded, set his book aside, stood and stretched his back, then returned to his position where anyone staking out the motel would have a clear enough view of him. If Tristan didn't know him, he'd buy the bored-front-desk-attendant-in-the-wee-hours-of-the-morning routine hook, line and sinker.

Noah scanned the bank of monitors, swiped a hand over his mouth and stood. "So, what's got you twisted up?"

Tristan shook his head, studied the motel parking lot, the T on the motel sign blinking on occasion as if it were about to give up. The road leading to the motel was empty. The woods surrounding it on three sides showed no activity, not even any stray rats rooting through the dumpsters. And then it hit him. "Why now?"

Noah frowned. "I don't follow."

Cayden propped a hip against the counter running the length of the box truck and scratched his head. "Me neither."

"When I was undercover with Rossi's organization, she roamed freely wherever she wanted." He struggled to pinpoint exactly what was bothering him and relay it in a way that would make Noah and Cayden see his concerns. "Gianna Rossi is the most arrogant woman I have ever met. She had no inhibitions. She did whatever she wanted, ran her crime ring like a business with an iron fist. And she never voiced any concerns about getting caught. At all. I never even saw a bead of sweat on that woman's brow. It was as if she thought she was untouchable."

Noah frowned and leaned closer to one of the monitors. "And now?"

"Back when we raided her offices, she should have been there." And yet, she wasn't. "She was always there."

"Until the night we went in," Cayden said, his tone neutral.

"Right. Exactly." And it had always bothered him. She should have been on-site, should have been present and arrested with the rest of her crew. But she'd somehow escaped their net. Escaped? Or been forewarned?

"We did an extensive internal investigation." Noah stuck his hands in his pockets, his gaze bouncing from one screen to the next, then rotating back through the routine again and again. "We never found any indication she had a mole in the unit."

"Then again, she still managed to get more than one agent on the inside and set off an incendiary device in front of our headquarters, then send people in with guns blazing to eliminate our witness." Cayden shrugged. "So, there's that."

Noah nodded thoughtfully.

"That's all true," Tristan said, "and it has always nagged at me that after all my careful planning, she still managed to escape." *Nagged at him* was too tame a phrase—it had eaten him up inside, kept him awake through more than one night, especially since her operation seemed to have continued, though he couldn't prove that. "But what's bothering me right now is the fact that she managed to avoid being seen anywhere since the raid. She went completely off the radar. And yet, now, out of nowhere, she shows up on a camera outside an airport in Rome, and then again here. What are the chances?"

Because it seemed too neat and tidy to him, as if…

"You think she meant to be seen."

It wasn't a question, which told him Noah had already pursued the same theory.

"She's taunting you, trying to lure you out." Cayden turned to scan the monitors.

Tristan nodded. Maybe, if that was true, it was a good thing. If she'd resorted to using herself as bait to draw him to her, it had to mean she didn't know where he was. Which meant Avery and Lily should be safe at the safe house. "Yeah, I think—"

Noah held up a hand, then pointed to a stand of trees at the far end of the motel parking lot on one of the screens. “There. Did you see that?”

Cayden and Tristan both leaned closer and studied the shadow he’d pointed out.

“Movement.” Noah hit the button on his shoulder to connect with their agent inside the motel lobby. “Get out.”

It was all he had time for before an explosion blew up on the screens and shook the truck, even from a block away.

Tristan flung the back door open and launched himself out before the truck even stopped rocking, weapon drawn. No way was he letting anyone get away this time.

Automatic gunfire brought him up short, peppering the back of the truck, shattering the surveillance equipment.

He dropped to his belly, scrambled toward cover. They’d been made. He should have known, should have realized Gianna wouldn’t fall for the ruse—might have if his head hadn’t been so wrapped around Avery and Lily.

Tristan returned fire even as he sought cover behind the Suburban. His first thought was to scan the night for Noah and Cayden. He’d seen Cayden crouch and run right behind him, but he hadn’t seen Noah emerge from the truck. Had he been hit?

He scanned the wooded area across the street where the gunfire had come from, flared his senses.

Cayden glanced at him from where he’d crouched behind the tire of an SUV.

Tristan shook his head. He didn’t know if the gunman was still out there. Silence resonated through the early-morning darkness, echoes of gunfire lingering in the hot, humid air. He had to find Noah, had to get to the motel, had to see if the agent who’d been in the lobby was all right. He had to get back to Avery and Lily. Because their plan had failed, and those he cared for were probably in more danger now than ever.

Cayden gestured for him to provide cover.

Tristan stood enough to aim his weapon over the hood of the Suburban while Cayden slid into the SUV, cranked the engine and pulled up, blocking the open back of the truck.

Noah jumped into the back seat, and Tristan breathed a sigh of relief.

Cayden shot forward until he was beside Tristan, then screeched to a stop, blocking the shooter's view. Keeping his head down, he shoved the passenger door open. "Get in!"

As Tristan lunged for the SUV, he heard the unmistakable sound of a car door slamming shut not too far in the distance, followed by the squeal of tires. He jumped in, and before he could get the door shut, Cayden rocketed out of the lot and down the road toward the motel.

"You both okay?" Tristan spared a quick glance over his shoulder at Noah.

Noah nodded. "Took two in the chest but, thankfully, I was already wearing my vest."

The bruises were probably already forming and throbbing, but it would have been so much worse if he hadn't had the bulletproof vest on. Tristan uttered a silent prayer of thanks, surprised at how easily and naturally the impulse came. Avery was right. It did feel better to pray as a first instinct. "The agent at the motel?"

"He's out. Injured, but he should be okay." Noah gestured toward Tristan's arm and tossed him a T-shirt from the back seat beside him. "How bad?"

He glanced at the flesh wound on his upper arm and

took a moment to press the shirt against it to stop the bleeding, mostly so his hand wouldn't be slick. "Just grazed."

Noah's cell phone rang, and he answered on speaker, then they all listened together to the update. No one had been killed at the motel; the only injury was to the agent playing desk clerk, and they'd apprehended a suspect fleeing the scene.

A wave of relief surged through him.

Bad news—the suspect wasn't Gianna Rossi.

They needed to put an end to Rossi's reign of terror—tonight, before anyone else got hurt.

Noah disconnected the call just as a dark-colored sedan fishtailed from a dirt road to their right onto the road in front of them, spewing up a cloud of dust in its wake.

Cayden didn't even slow.

When Tristan tried to lean forward, as if that would get him any nearer to the fleeing suspects, the seat belt caught and yanked him back. "Can you get any closer?"

Cayden pressed harder on the accelerator.

Noah clicked his seat belt into place, then put his phone against his ear and spoke quietly.

Tristan shoved everything else from his mind and focused on the vehicle ahead of them. He could see two heads in the car, and since the sounds of the door slamming and the car accelerating had come within a fraction of a second of each other, he had to assume their shooter was the passenger. So, who was driving?

Despite Cayden flying down the treacherous mountain road, the car in front of them eased ahead, increasing their lead.

Every nerve ending vibrated, sizzling like live wires,

begging him to get closer, to catch up to the vehicle, to apprehend the occupants. "Cayden…"

"Yeah. I know." He stomped on the gas, lost sight of the sedan as it rounded a curve ahead of them, then skidded around the same curve practically on two wheels. Thankfully, he had to hit the brakes to keep them from tumbling over the side, or they'd have broadsided the sedan as it spun out and rocked to a stop blocking the road.

The driver aimed an automatic weapon out the window and opened fire.

Tristan held his breath and kept his head low as Cayden skidded to a stop, fishtailing so the passenger side faced the vehicle. Then he fired through the shattered passenger window.

Noah fired from the window behind him, even as the passenger bailed out of the sedan and started through the woods up the mountain. No way were these two getting away.

"I hit the driver. The passenger fled on foot." And with that, Tristan was out of the SUV and running after the perpetrator. He tore past the driver, who'd fallen slumped over the steering wheel. Noah or Cayden would deal with him.

Tristan dug deeper, searching for more speed, as he vaulted a downed tree and kept going, barely keeping the dark-clad figure in sight. "Freeze! Police!"

The figure stopped and whirled to face him, then flashed a familiar grin, the same grin she'd been wearing when he'd watched her shoot a man in cold blood. Then Gianna Rossi opened fire.

Tristan dropped behind a rotted stump that wouldn't offer much protection and aimed. "Freeze, Gianna. There's nowhere to go!"

"There's always a way out. You should know that," she yelled back as she disappeared behind a thicket.

He had to locate her, couldn't risk losing her in the dark and giving her the chance to ambush him. If he could keep her talking…

"I should have known you couldn't resist the urge to be here." He scrambled away the instant the words left his mouth, was repositioned by the time she took her next shot.

"And miss taking you out myself? Not a chance." She'd crept to the left. "And you're right. You should have known. You should have known I'd go after those you love, too, but that didn't stop you from leaving them unprotected, did it?"

He clenched his jaw tight, trying to ignore the taunts no doubt designed with the hope he'd give away his position as well. He moved to his right, just enough to keep him from being in her crosshairs, then he adjusted his aim, searched the shadows for any sign of movement.

"I guess that's what happens when your family's in danger," she pressed. "You get stupid. And weak."

"Think again, Gianna. You made a mistake threatening my family. It only made me more determined to take you down. You won't get that chance again."

"We'll see about that." She stepped out from behind her cover and opened fire.

He dropped to the ground, getting a face full of dead leaves, pine needles and dirt. Better than a bullet.

Ignoring the sharp sting where one of her bullets grazed his temple, Tristan held his breath, calmly aimed, then squeezed the trigger.

Gianna went down.

He scrambled to his feet and ran to her, weapon held ready.

When he reached her, he found her lying in a bush where she'd fallen. He kicked her gun aside and leaned over to pat her down for more weapons.

Her dark eyes stayed trained on him, filled with defiance despite the fact that she lay caged among the thicket branches with a bullet wound to her chest. Apparently, she hadn't bothered with a vest. Her ego probably wouldn't allow her to even consider the fact that she might be defeated. Or, perhaps she'd rather go down than be taken alive.

Her breathing had turned rapid, and she sucked in shallow breaths, still grinning up at him.

There was so much he wanted to say to her. He wanted to yell, to scream, to threaten her for going after his family. He wanted to assure her she could never harm them again. He wanted to wipe that grin off her face. He still held the weapon trained on her. A tremor coursed through his arm, his hand. He swallowed hard, forced down the rage and holstered his weapon. "Turn over. You're under arrest."

She laughed as he yanked her out of the bush and rolled her over onto her stomach, blood streaming from the wound in her chest.

Would she make it? He had no idea, but he couldn't try to assess her condition or administer aid until he had her secured. This was one woman he would not underestimate. Not again.

He knelt, one knee on her back, and snapped the cuffs onto her wrists behind her, then rolled her onto her back again so he could see what damage had been done.

"You think you're so smart, don't you, McAvoy?"

Hearing her use his real name, even though he knew she'd discovered his true identity, had his blood running cold. Or perhaps that was shock. How badly had he been hit? He glanced down at the wound on his arm. Blood ran down and dripped from his fingers, but the wound didn't seem too deep. He pressed his fingers against his temple, and they came away bloody. He ignored it. "You have the right to remain silent."

"Now, sweetie, why would I want to do that?" She laughed, then choked, and blood sprayed from between her lips.

He refused to let her bait him. "You have the right to an attorney."

"I am an attorney, remember?" Her voice trailed off, and he missed the rest of what she said.

He leaned closer, tilting his ear toward her mouth. "Say that again."

"I said, you think you've won, but you haven't. He's got them even as you're here on your knees gloating."

Everything in him went completely numb. She had to be lying.

"Your only chance will be to make a trade…" *wheeze, wheeze* "…me for…" *wheeze* "…them." And then her eyes fluttered shut. "You'd better pray…" she coughed "…you can keep me…alive."

NINE

When the words in the book she'd sat staring at blankly for the past two hours started to blur, Avery squeezed her eyes closed and let the tears roll down her cheeks. Still, she held the book in front of her where she sat wrapped in a blanket in the chair beside the window, curtains drawn tight to block any view inside.

Then the now-familiar scene began to replay in her mind again, and her eyes shot open. She might as well give up, though, since there was little chance the kiss she'd shared with Tristan would leave her mind any time soon. The instant his lips met hers, five years had melted away and he was the same guy she'd loved all over again. Because with that kiss, all the love she'd felt for him had slammed back into her. There was no denying it. And when he returned…

"Oh, God, please let him return," she whispered softly.

Because, when he did, she was going to tell him the truth. She loved him with all her heart. She wouldn't deny it any longer. She couldn't. She had no idea what they'd do with it, or if Tristan felt any of the same things she did, but she owed it to him to be honest. If friendship was all he could give her, she'd have to accept that, but she wanted so much more.

She sniffed, swiped at her raw cheeks and scanned the small round table next to her for tissues. All she found was an empty box.

Bang! Bang! Bang!

She jumped, startled.

"Open the door! It's Sheriff Reynolds!"

Fear seized her as she dropped the open book, jumped out of the chair and tripped over her own feet trying to untangle herself from the blanket.

"We have a situation!" The sheriff pounded again.

When she started toward the door, Bella grabbed her arm. She shook her head, put a finger in front of her lips, then released her grip on Avery and bolted for the window.

"Avery, open the door. We have to get you and Lily out of here," the sheriff called.

Bella pointed to Lily as she yanked the curtains open.

Avery frowned at her but scooped Lily out of the bed and cradled her close.

The little girl startled awake and began to cry softly. "Mama?"

"It's me, Lily," Avery whispered against her ear.

"I need my blankie." She squirmed and reached toward the bed, knocking Avery off balance.

"I need you to stay very quiet, baby." She steadied herself with a hand on the mattress, then grabbed the blanket and thrust it into Lily's hands. "Can you do that?"

Three pops that sounded like gunfire had her heart skipping a beat, then beating painfully against her ribs.

Lily's eyes went wide, and she stuck her thumb into her mouth, clutched the blanket against her face and nodded.

By the time Avery shoved her feet into her sneakers, Bella had already thrown the window wide-open.

"I don't understand. What's happening?" Avery whispered.

"Tristan's been shot, Avery, and the safe house is no longer secure," Reynolds yelled through the door. "We have to go. Open up."

Tristan! She started for the door.

Bella once again grabbed her and shook her head insistently.

Avery stopped in her tracks. If Tristan had been shot, surely Bella would have been the first one notified. *Think, think, think.* "I'll be right there!" she yelled. "I'm just getting dressed."

"We go with no one but one of our team members." Bella draped one leg over the sill and out the window. "That's it. No exceptions."

"But—"

"No exceptions, Avery. Those are my orders." Bella dropped out the window, pressed her back against the side of the house and drew her weapon, then scanned the area and turned back. After a moment, she stuffed the gun back into its holster. "Hand Lily out to me."

There was no mistaking the automatic weapon fire from the hallway just outside the bedroom door. The safe house must be under attack. Was the sheriff really trying to get them to safety? Maybe it was Bella she shouldn't trust. But Tristan trusted Bella. And Avery trusted Tristan. She had to. There was no other choice. "Do you really think something happened to Tristan?"

"Avery, listen to me. I don't know. And that's honest. But we need to go."

Something crashed hard against the door. "Avery!"

"Now!" Bella stood on tiptoes and reached up. "Give her to me, then climb out. We'll cut across the clearing into the woods, then circle around and try to get to the SUV."

When Avery tried to hand Lily out to Bella, Lily threw her arms around Avery's neck and clung tight enough to cut off the circulation, making her light-headed. "Lily. You have to let go. I'll be right behind you."

"Noo!" she wailed. "Mama!"

"Lily, you have to shush. Please." Desperate to get Lily out before whoever was banging on the door could get in, Avery reached behind her and tried to unclasp her hands.

Something hit the door again, harder this time, and it splintered.

"What about Storm!" Lily yelled.

Sheer terror gripped Avery, squeezed, threatened to suffocate her. She had to get Lily somewhere safe. "Yes. Yes, baby. Bella's going to get the doggie. Go into her arms, and she'll take you to Storm and Tristan."

Still staring warily at her mother, Lily relinquished her hold and went to Bella.

Bella gave Avery a warning glare, but with Lily in her arms there wasn't much she could do.

The door cracked beneath the next blow. If Avery followed them out the window, they'd be caught for sure.

"Go! Now! You keep her safe, Bella!" As Lily's screams split the night, Avery slammed the window closed, locked it and yanked the curtains closed. She barely managed to scramble across both beds before the door gave way and slammed hard against the wall.

Sheriff Reynolds burst through the shattered door, gun aimed at her.

Avery dived into the bathroom screaming, "Keep her in the tub, Bella, and get down," then slammed the door shut behind her and locked it. She climbed onto the counter and stood, sucking in gulps of air, searching desperately for something she could use as a weapon. Hopefully, if the sheriff started shooting, he'd think she'd taken cover low, maybe in the tub where she prayed he believed Bella and Lily to be. The door wouldn't hold long, but it would have to be long enough for Bella to escape. Getting Lily to safety was all that mattered.

Right now, though, she had to put everything else out of her mind. No easy task when she had no idea if Lily or Tristan were safe, if they were even alive, but she wouldn't make it back to them if she didn't get her wits about her.

Bella clearly didn't trust Sheriff Reynolds. Was that just a precaution, or did she suspect he was loyal to Gianna Rossi? He could've either been blackmailed or threatened. Either way, if true, it didn't bode well for her. She needed something to fight back with. The countertop was clear save for a bottle of hand soap beside the sink. The tub was empty but for the bottles of shampoo and conditioner and a bar of soap. She was in some serious trouble.

She pressed her ear against the top of the door. Had Reynolds realized she'd been bluffing and gone after Lily instead? Or was he just being cautious because he knew Bella was armed? Or, could there still be a thin sliver of hope he hadn't sold out to Rossi and was on their side?

She held her breath, flared her senses, listened…and heard his harsh breathing beside the door. It wouldn't be long before he figured out he'd been duped. Once he tried to get in and didn't encounter gunfire, would he still try for her or abandon her and go after Lily? She couldn't wait around to find out.

She leaned over, slid a drawer open as quietly as possible. Nothing but a hair dryer. *Oh, God, please help me.*

The sheriff kicked the door. "If you open the door and

come out, Avery, I'll leave the kid behind. I'm sorry, I'll have to kill the agent, but you have my word I won't harm the girl. Backup will arrive soon enough and find her. If you come out now, there's a good chance she'll make it. If you make me bust this door down and haul you out, I will take her out with the agent."

Rage overtook the fear. How dare he! And to think she'd tried to hold on to hope of his innocence. She spotted a metal towel bar on the wall. It would have to do. She hopped down lightly, ripped the towels off the bar, then grabbed hold and braced her foot against the wall. She pulled with all her might. It might have loosened, but she couldn't be sure.

Something hit the door again, rattling it in the frame.

She wiggled the bar, braced herself, readjusted her grip and yanked as hard as she could. When the bar gave way, she tumbled to the floor, smacking her head against the vanity.

The door splintered, and the sheriff rushed in, firing at the empty tub. So much for not harming Lily.

Rage propelled her toward him, and she hooked his ankle and yanked it up, knocking him off balance.

He kept firing into the ceiling as he went down on his back.

Avery wound up as she shot to her feet, then swung the bar, hitting him squarely in the wrist. She caught his cheek on the backswing.

He managed to maintain his hold on the weapon as he rolled and regained his footing.

There was no way she could beat him. Instead, she ran. She didn't have much of a head start as she bolted through the room and down the hallway. The sight of several people down, not only FBI agents but some of the sheriff's own deputies as well, begged her to stop. Her heart broke when she spotted Oliver among those who'd been shot. Dead? She didn't know.

She resisted the urge to squeeze her eyes closed and kept running through the living room. She jumped over another downed agent and kept going. As much as she wanted to stop and check if anyone was alive, she couldn't. She had to keep moving.

"It's a good thing she needs you alive!" Reynolds raged from way too close behind her.

She burst through the front door. The hot, sticky air slammed into her chest and had her lungs begging for a full breath. She didn't dare pause. She fled down the steps, tripped and went down on her hands and knees on the pavers. The metal towel rod clattered away.

She struggled to get her feet beneath her, to reach the bar.

Reynolds grabbed her hair, yanked her up. He pressed the gun against her temple.

Still she fought, clawing at his face. Hadn't he said he needed her alive? She kicked, punched, tried to draw enough breath to scream. Her lungs ached, pleaded for air. Would anyone even hear her?

Then he slammed her head against a wooden post.

Pain radiated through her head. Her vision blurred.

"Just for that..." Sheriff Reynolds swiped an arm across his face, smearing blood up his cheek. Then he spat. He sucked in a few deep breaths. "Just for that, when she's done with you, I'll kill you myself."

His fist connected hard with her temple. Blackness encroached, tunneling her vision. "And when I'm done with you, I'll go get that little brat of yours, too. Just for fun."

She used the last of her strength to kick out, landed a good blow to the side of his knee.

He started to go down, caught himself against the railing and hit her again.

Her last thoughts were of Lily, then Tristan. It hadn't escaped her notice that Reynolds hadn't threatened him as well. Because he was already dead? *I'm sorry, Lily. I never would have left you for any other reason but to save you.* And she prayed Bella had escaped with Lily and that Tristan was still alive as everything went black.

Tristan's cell phone signaled a text as he strode down the hospital corridor toward Gianna Rossi's room. If Noah had word on the situation at the safehouse, he'd have called. So he ignored it, lest Noah have a change of heart and order him to leave the hospital. Or worse, report directly to the ER to have his own injuries tended to before checking and reassuring himself that Rossi was still in custody. Well, he respected his boss more than anyone he knew, would even consider him a friend, but no way was that happening.

Gianna had told him her men had Avery and Lily and that he'd be expected to make a trade. Was she telling the truth? Whatever was wrong at the safehouse preventing anyone from answering their calls, he could only pray Oliver and Bella had been able to protect Avery and Lily. But, since they couldn't contact anyone, and more agents hadn't yet arrived on scene to confirm or deny, he had to assume Rossi's threats were true. And the best way, the only way, to keep his family alive was to stay next to Gianna Rossi.

After spending a year hunting that woman down, then having her go after Avery and kidnap Lily, he couldn't entrust her to anyone else. He'd stand guard himself for however long was necessary if that's what it took to be sure she couldn't escape or contact anyone and send them after his family again, if she hadn't already succeeded in grabbing them. Even though Sheriff Reynolds had a deputy on her door and two inside her room, Tristan didn't trust too many people right now. And those he did trust were with Avery and Lily, on their way to the safehouse, or investigating and collecting evidence from the mess at the motel. Or…

He couldn't think about what might have happened to them if Rossi's men had somehow gotten through. Bella and Oliver would have died trying to protect his family. His breathing hitched. *God, please don't let that be what happened.*

Of course, he already knew from experience that Rossi always had a contingency plan in place. The thought prickled his already-raw nerves. There was nothing he could do about that until he could interrogate her. But, while Noah had agreed to allow him to go to the hospital and stand guard, he'd forbidden him to speak to her. And he was right, which Tristan knew on every level. If he intervened, it could wreck the entire case against her. Still…

"God, please, give me the strength to stand back and do nothing. For now," he whispered softly.

Storm glanced up at him and whined.

"I know, boy. It's okay. We'll get to rest soon, and we'll put all this behind us." He'd begun to find his way back to God, back to his faith, so why, as he strode down the quiet corridor with his own footsteps echoing back at him and Storm's claws tapping against the tile, did he feel so utterly alone? Perhaps because everyone he'd ever loved was lost to him—his parents, Avery, Lily, even Benny, who'd died because of Tristan's mistakes. Maybe him being alone was best for everyone he loved, since being with him only put them in danger.

Before he could delve deeper into that thought, his cell chirped again. He called Storm to halt, nodded to the deputy guarding Rossi's room, then peered through the small window on the door.

Gianna lay in the bed, eyes closed, both wrists cuffed to the railings. No phone sat on the table beside the bed, since Noah had ordered the landline removed. They'd taken her cell phone from her after placing her in custody, not that they'd been able to access it. The curtains were closed tightly across the windows. And two deputies stood guard, one on either side of the bed but far enough away that she wouldn't be able to reach them before they could draw their weapons if she did manage to escape. They weren't lounging in chairs, but standing at alert, seemingly ready for anything.

So, why was Gianna Rossi smirking?

And why did Tristan's stomach heave and turn over? He had no idea, but he'd seen that look on her face before, usually right before she cut someone down, in the instant that she realized she had the upper hand and knew she was going to come out on top.

He dragged his gaze from Rossi. He had to keep his focus, couldn't let her get inside his head. If he let his emotions guide him, he was going to make a costly mistake. Again.

He leaned his back against the wall and checked his texts. His heart stuttered at the unfamiliar number. Then he tapped the screen.

The first text was a picture of Avery lying in an open

car trunk, eyes closed, face battered. His heart stopped. He lurched away from the wall.

Storm barked as he scrambled out of the way.

How had they gotten to her? Were Oliver and Bella dead? And where was Lily? Did they have her? Had they already smuggled her out of the country? Or worse? No. He refused to believe they'd have killed her. Rossi was too greedy, and Lily would bring a high price. Rage ignited in him, then erupted, and he whirled toward Rossi's room.

"Uh, uh, uh. I wouldn't do that if I were you." The deputy sidestepped to block the door, weapon drawn, and gestured toward Tristan's phone.

He clutched it so tight he was surprised it didn't shatter, then lifted it and read the second text.

A simple trade. You for Avery. Hand your phone and gun to Deputy Pierce, and you have exactly fifteen minutes to get here before the offer expires. The text was followed by another with an address.

The deputy held out his free hand, gun still held ready. "Don't want to keep the man waiting. And don't even think about stopping to make a call. It takes exactly nine minutes and fifty-three seconds to get there. I've driven it myself several times. And it'll take at least four minutes to get from here to your car. Add the minute you'll spend deciding if you should go after the woman or try to keep Rossi from escaping, and you're cutting it awfully close. The clock starts now."

His blood boiled.

Pierce wagged his finger and grinned. "Tick tock."

In a fraction of a second, Tristan debated his options. Pull his gun and shoot the deputy, then contact Noah to get someone to the address? No time. They were at least ten minutes in the other direction. And he couldn't trust any of the sheriff's men. Ask a nurse or bystander to contact Noah on his way out? No way. It would take too long to convince someone to do as he asked, and he had no idea who to trust. Anyone could be on Rossi's payroll. He handed over his phone, pulled his weapon and gave the deputy that as well. "I'll be back for you."

"We'll be long gone by then." Pierce's laughter followed him down the hall.

It took less than the four allotted minutes to reach his SUV and get Storm loaded into the back. Still, no time to alert his team. If his team were all even still alive.

He tamped down the rush of grief. Would it once again be his fault a team member had been lost? He should have anticipated… Anticipated what? Rossi's reach? They already knew she had operatives in different law enforcement agencies, including their own, as well as several levels of government. That was how she commanded the resources she did. And he hadn't chosen Oliver and Bella for this assignment, Noah had. And still, that didn't lessen his guilt.

If he'd have just gotten back in touch with Avery any one of the numerous times she'd reached out, if he hadn't been such a coward, none of this would have happened.

And what of Gianna Rossi? Would her operation still be up and running at full capacity if he hadn't gone undercover? It seemed it was anyway. No matter how many operatives they took off the board, she seemed to have an endless supply with which to replace them.

He turned onto a deserted, mile-long dirt road headed up the mountainside, spraying plumes of dust behind him. There was no sense in trying to go in stealthily, since they already knew exactly when to expect him. As he entered a clearing, he spotted two men with automatic weapons standing guard on either side of the small cabin's front door. It seemed more like a hunting cabin, two, maybe three, bedrooms, probably an open living room–kitchen layout. Four windows across the front. Wide porch. Maybe a back door, no way to tell.

A quick scan of the area didn't offer many options for escape. The cabin was surrounded on three sides by thick forest; a fast-flowing river blocked any route out the back—close, from the sound of it. Even if he could rescue Avery and get out of the cabin, there was nowhere to run.

He unlocked his glove compartment and took out a backup handgun as he braked. But where could he conceal it? He had no doubt they'd search him before he ever made it inside. He turned the SUV until it faced the road, out of habit more than any sense of optimism that they'd be able to escape.

The men on the porch watched him closely but made no move to approach.

Tristan reached over to the back seat and grabbed Storm's work vest. As he stepped out of the SUV, he stuffed his gun into one of the side pockets. Maybe they'd check, and maybe they wouldn't, but at least he would have tried. Which Rossi would most likely expect.

He shook off the nerves, shoved all feelings aside and worked to concentrate on what he knew of Rossi. He'd been part of her organization for two years. He knew this woman, knew how she reacted. And so far, if he was being honest, she hadn't done anything he shouldn't have anticipated. Then again, if she truly had gotten married, and her husband really was worse than her, he had no idea what might come next.

He scanned the area as he opened the hatchback. "Storm, come."

The big dog jumped out and waited while Tristan secured the vest that would let Storm know he was in work mode.

He briefly debated leaving Storm in the SUV, but the night was too hot. He'd have left him behind if there had been time, but there hadn't. And he wouldn't leave Storm outside with two armed men. Besides, Storm was his partner. He'd have his back, as Tristan would always have his. "Heel."

He climbed the front porch, then lifted his arms when the two men moved to block the door.

One of them held his weapon trained on Tristan while the other patted him down. Apparently satisfied he'd left his own weapons behind, he stepped back, opened the door and gestured for Tristan to enter.

A small spark of hope tried to flare. If Rossi had been present and witnessed her guard allowing the dog to pass without being searched, she'd have eliminated him on the spot. She didn't believe in second chances. Maybe her husband, or whoever was running this show, wasn't quite as clever.

He stepped directly into the living room, its furnishings more luxurious than he would have expected. A rustic area rug covered a large section of the darkly stained barn-wood floors. An abundance of throw pillows in creams and rusts was piled on the deep green sectional with an oversize, matching ottoman that took up much of the space. If not for the armed gunmen standing on either side of the room, it would have been quite cozy.

Then a door opened, and Sheriff Reynolds stepped into the living room from what appeared to be a bedroom, judging by the quick glance Tristan was able to get before he shut the door behind him. Was Avery inside? "Tristan. I'm sorry it had to come to this. I really am."

"I don't understand." But he was afraid he did.

Reynolds shook his head, propped his hands on his hips, close to the weapon holstered there. "You can't say you weren't warned. All you had to do was heed that warning and everyone would have been safe. No one would have had to be hurt."

Tremors ran through him, and he struggled to maintain his composure. Was Reynolds Rossi's new husband? Or was he simply another hired henchman to do her bidding? Then he decided he really didn't care. Nothing else mattered right now except getting Avery to safety and finding out where Lily was. Then, once they were both safely tucked away, he would spend the rest of his life hunting down Gianna Rossi, Sheriff Reynolds and every single person who was loyal to them and making sure he brought each and every one of them to justice. He was foolish to ever have thought there was a chance of a happily-ever-after for him, Avery and Lily, but he would see to it that Avery and Lily got theirs. "Where is Avery?"

"She's alive, if that's what you're worried about. I held up my end of the bargain."

Tristan spread his hands wide, bringing his right hand within reach of the weapon in Storm's vest. "And I kept mine."

Reynold's nodded to one of his associates. "Enzo, bring the woman."

The guy left, but instead of heading into the room Reynolds had come from, he walked out the front door, where at least two more gunmen stood guard.

Sweat beaded on Tristan's brow, stung his eyes. He

didn't dare wipe it away, needed both hands free. This might be the only chance he'd have.

Storm, trained to assess body language and cues, kept his gaze riveted to the man holding the weapon, fidgeting back and forth. If Tristan gave the attack command, Storm would go for the gunman rather than Reynolds, who held no weapon, stood casually at ease and spoke in conversational tones.

Tristan inhaled, slow, deep, careful not to give anything away. He couldn't risk having Avery in the cross fire. He had to take Reynolds out now.

He blew out the breath, braced himself…

"I should have done away with you back then, you know. When I took care of your parents," Reynolds said.

Tristan froze. "What did you just say?"

"They couldn't mind their own business, either. Ever the do-gooders." He shook his head, grinned, but kept his dark eyes glued to Tristan, wary enough to know he was provoking a competent opponent. "When a child went missing, your father and your mother joined the search party, like the respectable citizens they were. Imagine my irritation when the two of them stumbled upon the place I had her stashed."

Tristan's hands started to shake first, then the tremors spread throughout his body.

"She was worth too much for me to let them take her home." He chuckled, his expression holding no humor. "Plus, there was no way I'd risk earning Gianna Rossi's wrath. I've seen firsthand how that woman handles incompetence. No, thank you."

Tristan couldn't breathe. He tried to inhale, couldn't fill his lungs. All these years he'd thought Reynolds was simply incompetent, that his parents had been the unfortunate victims of a random mugging. And all along, it had been Reynolds who'd killed them, the man he'd called regularly for updates on an investigation that would never have been solved.

A mock shiver ran through the sheriff and he laughed. "Terrifying, really."

His chest burned, his lungs begging for air.

"Anyway, I just wanted to make sure you knew Avery and Lily weren't the only two I'd taken from you." His grin turned ice-cold. "And make no mistake, neither of them will live."

He finally gasped in a breath.

"Oh, don't look so surprised. Lying is the least of my sins."

Tristan staggered, stumbled, started to go down.

Reynolds laughed. "You know what—"

He grabbed the gun from Storm's vest. "Bite!"

A blur of black in his peripheral vision, followed by the gunman's screams as Storm latched on to his wrist and bit down hard enough to keep him from firing his weapon, assured him Reynolds could be his priority. "Freeze, Reynolds!"

The sheriff's gaze shifted from Storm shaking his massive head back and forth while the gunman tried to fight him off to Tristan holding his gun aimed right at him. Then he reached for the weapon holstered at his side.

"Don't do it, Reynolds!" He didn't want to shoot him. He wanted him to go to prison for the rest of his life.

Reynolds hesitated.

"On your knees." If he could restrain these two before the other gunman returned or the two on the porch heard the scuffle—or worse, a gunshot—he might still be able to save Avery and Lily. If the others knew he'd gotten the upper hand, they'd surely either kill them or take them and flee. He was running out of time. "Last chance. On your knees. Now!"

Reynolds went for the weapon, yanked it from the holster and lifted it toward Tristan.

Tristan fired, and the sheriff went down. Tristan ran to him, secured the weapon and checked for a pulse. Reynolds wouldn't be facing justice in this world.

He turned to the gunman, still grappling with Storm, and reached to disarm him.

The sound of a gunshot echoed an instant before a spot of blood blossomed on the gunman's forehead, his eyes went wide, and he crumpled to the floor beside Reynolds. Then a man's voice spoke calmly. "Storm, release!"

Storm instantly released his hold and stepped back.

Confused, since Storm should only follow his handler's commands, Tristan whirled toward the voice behind him.

"It's good to see you, Tristan. Sorry about having to kill him, but Gianna doesn't suffer those who can't do their jobs properly." Benny Regan stepped past him, petted Storm's head and leveled his gun casually toward Tristan. "So, how are you? It's been a long time."

TEN

Avery stumbled when the gunman shoved her through the front door, flung a hand out blindly and caught herself against a sturdy, waist-high entryway table just in time to keep from going down. She blinked, then squinted against the sudden brightness of the room after spending who knew how many hours in the dark trunk of a black sedan, partial license plate HLC… It was all she'd seen, but she'd committed it to memory and reminded herself at every opportunity. *H-L-C, hug Lily close.* Her determination to pass the information on to Tristan helped her cling to some small tether of hope that she might yet escape this nightmare. She also had to let him know Sheriff Reynolds was involved. But he'd crushed her cell phone so she couldn't be tracked before he'd dumped her in the trunk.

"Keep moving." A not-so-gentle prod with the barrel of a very big gun accompanied the gunman's gruff command.

She lifted her gaze, and everything tried to register at once. Sheriff Reynolds and another man lay unmoving on the floor, and Tristan stood nearly toe to toe with a man she'd never seen before. She could only see Tristan's profile, but his mouth hung open as if shocked.

"I'm afraid I'm going to need you to hand that gun

to Enzo." The man stood with one hand aiming a gun at Tristan's chest and the other on Storm's head.

But that didn't make sense. Why would Storm be standing so at ease with a gunman threatening Tristan? Had Tristan ordered him to do so?

The man stepped back and waved his weapon for Enzo to put her beside Tristan and take the weapon from Tristan's hand.

Once Tristan had been disarmed, she stood next to him, tremors coursing through her entire body, desperately trying to resist the urge to reach out to him lest he need his hands free to fight.

The stranger grinned at Tristan. "Aren't you going to introduce me to the mother of your child?"

Tristan clenched his jaw so tight she was surprised his teeth didn't shatter.

"No? How rude," the man goaded. Then he shrugged and turned to Avery. "Allow me to introduce myself then. Benny Regan. Sorry to meet under such…well…less-than-ideal circumstances."

Benny Regan? She knew that name. Wasn't that Tristan's colleague? "But I thought you were dead."

"Ah, that. Yes, so, it seems, did the rest of the world. A rather dangerous assumption. Shall we say, rumors of my demise were largely exaggerated. I simply disappeared to follow my passion. And my wife would never have killed me."

Tristan stiffened beside her, then stood perfectly still, practically pulsating with what she could only assume was rage. Not that she could blame him.

She studied him in her peripheral vision, tried to gauge what he wanted her to do—fight? Run? But she couldn't get his attention. "You're married to Gianna Rossi?"

"That's right. Married in a secret ceremony in Rome months before Tristan's undercover operation ended."

Why wasn't Tristan saying anything? Too shocked? Hurt? Betrayed? While she could certainly understand all those feelings, surely he wasn't going to just stand there and let Benny shoot him. Right? Maybe he was just waiting for an opening, and that's why his attention was so riveted on Benny. She had to stall, had to give him time to either get over the shock or devise a plan of attack.

"I don't understand," she said.

Storm glanced back and forth between the two, probably just as confused as she was.

Benny leaned a hip against the back of the sectional, folded his arms across his chest with the gun held loosely, apparently satisfied Storm wouldn't attack and the other gunman would keep Tristan from making any move before Benny could react.

"Why did you let Tristan go if you were involved with Gianna's organization?" she asked.

"See, that's the thing about opportunity. When it knocks, you answer. Right, my man?" He wagged a finger at her then grinned, clearly enjoying Tristan's discomfort. "We allowed the raid to go forward, sacrificed the lower-level operatives we used to secure the offices, and tortured and killed one agent, leaving his body for you to find. Just to make things look legit, you know? But you'll be happy to know the other two missing agents are fine and happily in my employ. Then I slipped away to meet up with my wife. A win-win, really. Everyone thought I was dead. Gianna went off the radar and escaped the country on a private jet before the raid even began. The only thing that went wrong was… Tristan McAvoy."

She was going to have to do something. She was trying to wait, trying to follow Tristan's lead, but she sensed they were running out of time. She scanned the room, discreetly, she hoped, searching for anything she could use as a weapon. The ottoman had a wood tray that appeared pretty substantial, but it was too far away. No doubt she'd be gunned down before she made it. The fireplace tools were all the way across the room, so same problem.

Benny shifted his attention to Tristan then, gritted his teeth. Red patches stained his cheeks. "You were supposed to die that night. You never should have made it out of that office building alive. But the operative who was specifically tasked with killing you took off when he realized we intended to abandon all of them to be either killed or picked up by the police. It's not like any of them knew enough to hurt us, so they didn't matter. After all, sometimes you have to sacrifice a few pawns to protect the king and queen. Am I right?" He didn't wait for an answer. "Of course I am. I guess I don't need to tell you how that worked out for him."

Tristan spoke so softly Avery had to hold her breath to hear him. "You went after the woman I love…"

Avery couldn't help but notice he'd said *love*, not *loved.* Warmth spread through her chest, crept up, heated her cheeks. Probably not appropriate, considering the circumstances, but she barely managed to suppress a smile.

"You kidnapped my child," he spat.

That tossed ice water on her warm and fuzzies.

"Yes." Benny perked up, unclenched the fist he'd tightened. "Imagine my pleasant surprise when we uprooted a family connection. You, who was chosen for this assignment because you had no one, always so gung-ho to go it alone. For a brief minute in time, Gianna was actually concerned about you succeeding in taking us down."

She had to pull her attention away from Tristan, give him room to react. A freestanding lamp stood within reach, but it was plugged into an outlet in the floor. It might be usable as long as there was enough slack to allow her a good swing or the plug came free. Not ideal, nor guaranteed, but it might be her only option. Oh, well. She might go down, but at least she'd go down fighting. "But you weren't worried about him winning?" Avery asked.

"Not for a minute." Benny shifted his gaze to check his perfectly manicured nails, feigning disinterest even though his posture remained tense, as if daring Tristan to react.

Avery held her breath, but Tristan made no move, which was probably for the best considering Benny was no doubt baiting him. She wiped her sweaty palms on her leggings.

"I knew if we couldn't unearth anyone Tristan cared about, we could always use me as bait. If it leaked that I was alive, that I was being held hostage and tortured, Tristan would have come out of hiding to save me. Gianna was against it, of course. Didn't have the stomach to risk my life. But I had the tactical advantage. I knew the two things Tristan valued above all else..." He paused, looked Tristan directly in the eye and lifted a brow in challenge. "Friendship and loyalty."

The attack came hard and fast. One minute Tristan was standing a foot from Benny, the next he was on him.

Avery grabbed the lamp and swung as hard as she could just as the second gunman fired. She hit his shoulder, and the volley of shots went wide, tearing up the back of the sectional.

"Storm, bite!" Tristan yelled from where he fought Benny.

Benny clawed Tristan's face, trying desperately to free his gun hand, but Tristan maintained a rigid grip.

Storm launched himself at Enzo and tore into his wrist just as Avery swung the lamp back the other way. The lamp base struck the gunman's head, sending a reverberation all the way back up the pole and into her arms. Her grip loosened.

The gunman yanked the lamp from her hand, but with Storm shaking his head wildly back and forth with the man's wrist clutched between his sharp teeth, he was forced to release the lamp and let it clatter to the floor.

Leaving it where it landed, Avery lunged for Enzo's gun, wrestling it free from his hand slicked with blood. She leveled the weapon at him, eased her finger against the trigger. She blew out a slow breath. *Oh, God, please don't let me have to shoot anyone.* "Freeze!"

Enzo whirled toward her, one hand planted against Storm's head as he tried to pull his arm free. Then he went perfectly still, eyes wide.

"If you don't stop fighting and kneel on the floor, I will shoot you." True? She had no idea. If the tremors rocking her body to the point of nausea and the shakiness in her voice were any indication, probably not.

He shot his free hand in the air. "Get the dog off me!"

Unfortunately, she had no idea how to do that, and Tristan made no move to call him off. Of course, he was locked in a life-and-death struggle over the weapon clutched between him and Benny.

Thankfully, Storm maintained his grip but simply held still.

Avery lifted the weapon, her gaze torn between watching Enzo and keeping an eye on Tristan. She had to get Enzo subdued before the other two gunmen on the porch heard the battle. They hadn't come at the sound of gunshots, so clearly they'd expected them. Which told her all she needed to know. Benny had no intention of letting either of them walk out of there alive. "On your knees. Now!"

Enzo sobbed but dropped to his knees.

Storm stood rigid.

"Benny!" she yelled.

He paused, his attention diverted for a split second. But it was long enough.

Tristan swung hard, landing a fist against Benny's jaw, and he staggered back. Tristan hit him again, followed through once more and Benny fell, smacked his head against the stone hearth and lay still. A puddle of blood spilled onto the barn-wood floor surrounding his head.

Tristan relieved Benny of his weapon. "Keep that weapon aimed at Enzo, Avery, and if he even twitches, shoot him. Do you understand?"

Unfortunately, she did. She nodded, then firmed her expression, praying it would be enough to keep the guy where he was.

Tristan patted him down, pulled a handgun from a holster under his arm and a cell phone from his pocket. "Storm, release. Guard."

Storm obeyed the order instantly.

Tristan set Benny's and the other gunman's weapons on the kitchen island, then trained his own on Benny. He grabbed a knife from the block on the counter and returned, cut the cord from the lamp and rolled Benny over, then used it to bind Benny's hands behind his back before he could regain consciousness.

With Benny secured and Storm guarding the second gunman, who knelt on the floor cradling his bloodied hand against him, rocking back and forth and sobbing, Tristan peered out the front door, then closed it, locked it and called for backup. "The gunmen outside must have taken off."

As Avery's adrenaline rush subsided, the tremors increased, and her legs turned to rubber. It took every ounce of her strength to lock her knees and remain on her feet. She had to find Lily. With so many law enforcement agents on Gianna's payroll, what if Bella worked for her, too? What if she'd taken off with Lily or brought her to Gianna? Her breathing turned harsh, ragged, and she could barely suck in enough air.

And then Tristan was there, wrapping an arm around her and easing the weapon from her hands. "It's all right, honey. You can let it go. I have you now."

"Tristan..." The sob escaped before she could stop it. "Did Bella get Lily to you? Is she okay?"

"She's fine. When I called Noah for backup, he said an EMP knocked out communications, so Bella couldn't call in and had to walk halfway down the mountain with her before she could get help. But Bella got her out, and they have her."

And then her legs did give out. If not for Tristan, she'd have gone down when they buckled. He pulled her against him, wrapped his arms around her, cradled her head against his chest. "Shh. It's over now."

"What about Gianna?"

He shrugged against her. "I don't know. She was at the hospital when I left. The deputy on the door was on her payroll, but I don't know about the two in the room with her. I relayed everything to Noah, and he's on his way here. I have no doubt he'll have answers when he gets here, one way or the other."

Avery nodded, then let it drop. Right now, all she wanted was Tristan's arms around her. She'd thought for sure Benny was going to kill him. And she realized she'd made a terrible mistake. She had no idea what the future would bring, what would happen with Gianna or any of her men that got away. All she knew was that she wanted Tristan in her life, in whatever capacity he would allow. She still loved him, with all her heart, and it had taken almost losing him to realize that. The past didn't matter, only the present. And the future.

She lifted her head. "Tristan."

He cradled her face between his hands and kissed her, not the long, deep kiss she craved, but a soft, gentle caress with the promise of more, which had her knees going weak once again. And then he pulled back and gave her the same boyish grin she remembered. "Before you say anything…"

Which was good, because whatever she'd been about to tell him seemed to have slipped away the instant his lips met hers again.

"There's something I need to ask you."

Tristan hesitated, not because he was uncertain about what he wanted—he'd never been more sure of anything in his life—but because he didn't know how Avery would react. And he couldn't stand the thought of leaving her again. He didn't know how they'd work out the logistics of it all, only that they would.

He tucked her hair behind her ear, searched her eyes and found the same love he'd first discovered there when they were teenagers, but with an intensity they hadn't known back then. He wanted to take her out of there, take her somewhere they could talk for hours. He wanted to hear everything about her and Lily's lives, needed to tell her so many things. But he couldn't, not until Noah and his team arrived and took over the scene.

That was okay, though, because he could tell her the one thing that mattered most. "I love you, Avery, with everything in me. I never stopped."

"I love you, too, Tristan." A tear slid down her cheek. "I always have."

"Avery…" He caught the tear with his thumb, kissed her again. "Will you marry me?"

"Seriously?" She laughed, closed her eyes and laid her head against his chest. "Only you would ask that under these circumstances."

He held her against him, reveling in the feel of her, reluctant to ever let her go. "I know it's not the romantic setting you deserve, but I don't want to take a chance of you coming to your senses and saying no."

She looked up, and a smile spread across her face. "Don't worry. There's no chance of that happening."

Everything in him settled. "Is that a yes?"

She nodded against him, then stepped back and met his gaze. "Yes, Tristan, I'll marry you."

"Good, because I was afraid I was going to have to beg." He traced a finger along her cheek, down her jaw, where bruises already mottled the skin. As much as it pained him to see them there, he knew they would heal. The injuries would heal. The trauma would heal. And they would become a true family, in every sense. "Because I can't live without you again, Avery."

"You don't have to."

And he couldn't live without his daughter, either. He pulled Avery against him, cradled her close, aware of her injuries. He had no clue what the future might hold for them, or how they would work things out. He only knew that together they would. And that was all that mattered.

"We're coming in, Tristan," Noah called through the front door an instant before the battering ram slammed it open. "You two okay?"

Perfect. Tristan nodded. "We're good."

"Good." Noah was already directing agents to secure the scene. "Because you have a visitor out here who's anxious to see her mama."

Avery jerked away from him and whirled toward the door. "Lily!"

"You go ahead, Avery, I'll be right behind you." The hardest thing he'd ever had to do was let go of her in that instant, but she needed to go to Lily, and there were still things he needed to wrap up. He watched her until she cleared the front door with Cayden beside her, then turned to Noah.

"I figured it was safest for now to keep her with us," he told Tristan.

Too choked up to answer, Tristan simply nodded. It was the right call, the only call, considering the chaos that would now have to be sorted out.

"We'll get this all figured out, Tristan. The worst of it is behind us."

And he trusted Noah wouldn't leave any stone unturned when it came to finding everyone who'd had any part in Rossi's organization. "Oliver?"

"He's alive, and he'll recover."

Tristan nodded, overcome with emotion.

Then Noah shot him a grin. "And already climbing the walls and telling anyone who'll listen that he wants out of the hospital."

Some of the tension eased from Tristan's taut muscles.

That sounded just like Oliver. He was almost afraid to ask, wanted to bask in the victory for just a few minutes before reality set in and robbed him of his relief, but he had to know. "And Gianna Rossi?"

Noah's expression turned hard. "We've still got her."

"Seriously?" Because he'd been sure she'd escape when he chose to go after Avery.

"Yup." Noah patted his back. "When the guard who took your phone and gun entered the hospital room to free her, one of the other guards took him out. Seemed the two men inside the room weren't on her payroll."

Storm trotted to Tristan, and he bent to ruffle his fur as he watched two agents lead Enzo from the room. "Good boy, Storm. You are such a good boy."

He couldn't fault Storm for following Benny's order. After all, he'd been trained to do so. Speaking of… He glanced at where Benny had fallen, where two paramedics appeared to be working to save him. While he was glad he hadn't killed him, it stung that Benny had deceived him, had been willing to use Tristan's loyalty against him. Still… Benny would have a long time to think about his mistakes when he got life in prison for the crimes he'd committed, starting with the murder of his own gunman.

But there would be time to brief Noah on that later. Now he needed to see his family. Leaving Noah to deal with the aftermath, he strode through the front door and down the porch steps to where Bella stood with Avery and Lily.

He hugged Bella, kissed her cheek, kept his arm around her for a moment. "Thank you for keeping Lily safe."

"I'm sorry about Avery. I couldn't—"

He held up a hand. "You have nothing to be sorry for.

I'm just glad you were able to get Lily away and you weren't hurt."

She nodded.

He gave her one last squeeze before turning to Avery.

She stood looking at him, Lily wrapped tightly around her, tears streaming down her cheeks.

When Lily lifted her head and spotted Storm, she flung an arm open to him. "Storm!"

Storm trotted to her and nuzzled against her.

She petted him for a moment, then lifted her gaze to Tristan and held out her hand.

He went to her, unsure how to proceed, way out of his element.

And then she wrapped her arm around his neck.

He hugged her and Avery tight, Storm nudging between them, and couldn't have been more grateful.

EPILOGUE

Avery held her breath as they rounded the last curve that would bring them back to the home she'd grown up in. What would it be like to come upon the house for the first time since Lily had been taken from it what seemed like a lifetime ago? Would she be able to relax there without reliving that scene over and over again?

Keeping one hand on the wheel, Tristan reached for her hand, entwined his fingers with hers and brought their joined hands to his lips. "It's going to be okay, Avery."

She smiled at him, the glint from her wedding ring a reminder of the promises they'd made.

Tristan had promised her that the house, which had been lost in the fire, would be rebuilt before the baby came, and he'd kept his promise. Barely.

When the baby kicked, apparently just as eager to see her new home as Avery was, she laid a hand on her belly.

"We're home!" Lily yelled and clapped her hands together.

Storm barked, and the black-and-white Landseer puppy followed suit as he jumped against the barrier between the cargo hold and the back seat.

"Down, Oreo!" Lily yelled and giggled at the puppy Tristan had gifted her when he and Avery had gotten married. He'd told her it was her very own partner who would always protect her, even when he and Storm had to go away for an assignment. And after that, the nightmares had started to ease, and she'd begun to heal. She'd taken his training seriously. It had surprised Avery that the pup listened so well to her, but Tristan had helped her train him, and the two had become inseparable.

Tristan pulled into the clearing out front and turned the car to face the house. Much of the surrounding land was still blackened from the fire, but over the past year, new growth had begun. He parked and sat, waiting for Avery to say something.

She studied the house. It was similar to the one she'd grown up in, but Tristan had insisted on subtle changes. The new house was larger, a two-story, farmhouse style with pale yellow siding and a wraparound porch that had changed the entryway, so it no longer resembled the spot where the gunmen had first confronted Avery.

Lily extricated herself from the car seat and bounced between Avery's and Tristan's seats. "Can me, Storm and Oreo go in?"

Tristan simply held Avery's hand and waited. As much as he'd wanted to return with her and Lily to their home, he'd promised her the choice would ultimately be up to her. They could always list this house for sale and return to the house they'd been renting in town since they'd gotten married until they could find something new.

Lily bounced up and down. "Let me out, Daddy!"

Avery couldn't help but smile.

Then she leaned over Avery's belly, rested her hand over her new sister and whined. "I want to show the new baby the house."

Tristan studied Avery across their children, patient, as always.

Avery cherished the moment with her husband, Lily, their unborn child and their two dogs, who were more family than pets. Then she took a deep breath and smiled as she tugged on his hand. "Come on. Let's go see our new home."

"Yay!" Lily clapped her hands together, then scrambled across Tristan's lap and out the door the instant he opened it.

His laughter warmed Avery's heart. The two had become so close since the events that had first thrown them together. While Tristan still worked for the Missing Persons Unit, even still traveled when necessary, he no longer took undercover assignments. A choice that had been his alone, though Avery couldn't deny being grateful.

And he'd finally begun to come to grips with the fact that Reynolds had murdered his parents. Attending church as a family, with the support of everyone in town, had helped him to heal. He'd even finally been able to visit their graves. Now it was time to leave the past behind them and move forward.

He followed Lily around the back, opened the hatchback to release the dogs, then opened Avery's door and held out a hand. "Ready?"

"Yup." She gripped his hand and climbed out, then simply stood staring at their new home while Lily and the dogs jumped and ran and played. It was the perfect yard to raise children, to give them space to grow and learn, as it had always been.

At first, she'd refused to even think about returning. But then she'd begun to miss her home on the mountainside. And Tristan had offered to remodel and rebuild something wonderful. It seemed he'd been true to his word.

She thought of her grandfather, the home filled with love he'd given her growing up, and she was so grateful—grateful Lily had been saved, grateful Tristan had returned to them, grateful for the new life they were ready to welcome. And she was happy.

She hooked her arm through Tristan's and kissed his cheek.

He grinned. "Not that I'm complaining, but what was that for?"

"Thank you." She lifted her chin toward the house so she wouldn't have to relinquish her hold on him. "It's perfect."

He released her just long enough to wrap his arm around her and tuck her close. "You know it's completely up to you, right? I'll be happy anywhere as long as I have you guys with me."

"I do, yes, and I can't tell you how much I appreciate that. But with her organization finally dismantled..." She wouldn't utter her name, not in front of her new home. That woman would never invade her life again. "...and her and her husband locked away for the rest of their lives, I'm ready to move on."

The FBI had made other arrests as well, and an investigation into the local sheriff's office had ensued. Shock had rippled through the small community after Reynolds was killed and again when word leaked that he was involved with the kidnapping ring and that several other deputies had been arrested. Tristan squeezed her close. "So, it's a yes?"

She grinned. The same question he'd asked her when he'd proposed amid a virtual battlefield. "It's a yes."

"Woot!" He offered a sly grin and gestured toward the road, where a couple of dark SUVs headed toward them. He'd thought having Noah, Val, Dr. Keller, Cayden, Bella and Oliver, who was still healing from his life-threatening injuries, over would help alleviate her fears, make her feel safe. Especially since they'd all become such close friends. "Good thing, because Lily and I invited some friends for a housewarming party."

Lily ran to her mother and father, skidded to a stop and bounced up and down with her arms in the air.

Tristan plucked her up, swung her high, then tucked her between them.

Storm sat beside them and barked toward the coming company, and Oreo danced around their feet.

Lily hooked one arm over Avery's neck and the other arm around Tristan's, hugging them close as she studied her new home. She kissed them each on the cheek in turn, then grinned. "Me, Oreo and the new baby love it here."

And Avery's heart burst with joy. There was nowhere in the world she'd rather be.

* * * * *

If you enjoyed this story,
Be sure to watch for more stories in
Deena Alexander's brand-new
Missing Person Investigations series!
Available only from Love Inspired Suspense!

Dear Reader,

Thank you so much for sharing Tristan and Avery's story! I love flawed characters, whose internal conflicts are as unique and challenging as the danger they find themselves in.

One of the things Avery struggles with is the ability to trust. Tristan hurt her in the past, and she has a difficult time learning to trust him again. I think all of us go through trials in our lives that make it difficult to open up and trust one another, but as long as we continue to trust in God, I believe we can learn to trust others—and maybe even ourselves—again.

As for Tristan, he finds it difficult to forgive himself. I often wonder why it's so much easier to forgive others than it is to forgive ourselves, but I'm glad Tristan found his way through and back to Avery and Lily.

I hope you've enjoyed sharing Tristan, Avery and Lily's journey as much as I enjoyed creating it. If you'd like to keep up with my new stories, you can find me on Facebook at DeenaAlexanderAuthor and Twitter at DeenaAlexanderA.

Or visit my website to sign up for my newsletter.

Deena Alexander